ALL IN HER HEAD

N.M. Cedeño

A Lucky Bat Book

All in Her Head
Copyright 2014 by N. M. Cedeño
All rights reserved
Cover Artist: Brandon Swann
Published by Lucky Bat Books

10 9 8 7 6 5 4 3 2 1
ISBN: 978-1-939051-79-0

This book also available in digital formats.
Discover other titles by the author at nmcedeno.com

Acknowledgements

Thank you, Laurel Clements and Deborah Dillon. You are the best second readers.

Chapter 1

After showering away any remaining splatters of blood, Martha left her apartment to drive to Parkland Memorial Hospital, hoping that the man was still alive. A low rumble from the sky diverted her attention as she locked her apartment door. Towering thunderheads blotted out the sun, darkening the sky to a foreboding gray. The police had told her that the man, named Curt Holliczek, had been taken to Parkland Memorial for treatment and that his wife had been contacted. If she wanted to know about his condition, she would have to go to the hospital and speak to his wife. The hospital would never tell her anything over the phone. Storm or no storm, she had to go.

A small knot formed in Martha's stomach as she drove. Traffic wasn't approaching rush- hour levels yet, but it was heavy enough to bother her. As she pulled into the hospital's visitor parking lot, small balls of rain, too big to call drops, began to pummel her car. By the time she bolted through the sliding-glass doors at the entrance of the hospital, the rain was coming down in a torrential curtain, and lightning danced between the roiling clouds.

Martha glanced at the clouds, pictured a tornado forming, and deleted the image from her mind. Her feet and brown leather sandals were soaked. Water dripped down her arms and spotted her green, denim dress in spite of her umbrella, which she shook out and closed. Jogging through the second set of automatic glass doors into a blast of freezing air-conditioned air, Martha immediately began to shiver. Her heavy, mahogany brown hair pulled into a low ponytail at the base of her neck (the only part of her that the umbrella had successfully protected) was still wet from showering.

At the lobby information desk, a stern-looking, gray-haired volunteer with a squashed nose like a Pekingese sat in front of a computer terminal. She was speaking into the phone, "One moment, please, and I'll connect you." She completed the transfer and turned her attention to Martha.

"How may I help you?"

Curt Holliczek's name stuck to Martha's tongue as she realized she hadn't brought a card. "Where's the gift shop?"

The volunteer rattled off directions. Martha found the shop, and browsed the "get well" card section. Most of the cards were too personal for her to give to someone she didn't know, which left the supposedly humorous ones as the only option. Martha chose the one that seemed the least cheesy. It wasn't the gift card industry's finest work, but it would do.

Dropping down into a hard plastic chair in the lobby, Martha pulled a pen from her bag. As she popped the cap on the back end of the pen, her mind began to run itself again.

What on earth do you write to someone who was shot right in front of you, who may now be dying? You don't know anything about him except that he was bleeding horribly and still had the presence of mind to worry about his baby. Please, God, help him. You could always say, "Get well soon," and leave it at that. Oh, yeah, sure, with the post script, "By the way, I'm the one who watched you get shot."

Martha tapped the pen on the armrest of the chair. The thoughts began to spin out of control, like a race car's tires at full speed. She tried to force the worst of them back as they came.

Why did you come? You don't know what to say or what to do. If his relatives are here, you'll be intruding.

Come on, I can do this. I'll hate myself if I don't let them know I care. I have nothing to apologize for. They might want a first-hand description of what happened. Maybe not now, but later they will. Especially if he dies. Which he won't. Please, God. I'll just leave my name and number and let them know I'm willing to talk to them.

She scrawled, "I'm praying you have a swift recovery. I wish I could have done more to help. Martha Rowan." She added her email address and cell phone number on the opposite page.

Forcing the card into the envelope, Martha squared her shoulders. She walked back to the information desk and asked for Curt Holliczek's room. Punching in the button for the floor on the elevator, Martha watched the doors close and exhaled deeply.

SHE REMEMBERED THE morning starting like all the others since she had moved to Dallas three months ago. The day began to replay in her head …

A blast of ozone, exhaust, and heat enveloped Martha as the doors opened in front of her that morning. She hopped off the DART train, crossed the street, and began to cut through a parking lot that was tightly packed with cars.

A blue minivan and a grime-encrusted, monster SUV were blocking her path back to the sidewalk. Martha hated walking between large vehicles. It felt unsafe, but the summer air was scorching, and the most direct route to her office lay between the large vehicles. She was approaching the SUV when a harsh voice rose from between it and the minivan.

"Give me your wallet and keys!"

Sandals skidding on the rough asphalt, Martha slammed to a stop. She jumped backward and dropped down, before inching forward to peek around the bumper of the SUV. A dark-haired man in blue jeans and a gray sport coat stood facing her. The barrel of a small gun protruded from his right hand. A stocky man with sandy hair stood between Martha and the gunman. He was facing the gunman with his hands raised defensively.

Crouching behind the filthy SUV, Martha whipped her head around, looking for help. Downtown Dallas was filling with people arriving for work, and everyone was going the wrong way. She could see the square glass solarium of the Dallas World Aquarium, surrounded at its base by incongruous, non-native, leafy, tropical plants, looming in the distance to her right. The aquarium was a tourist site, not open for another hour. To her left she could see the back of the DART West Transit Center. The transit center was probably full of people, but they were on the other side of the building. Calling 911 wasn't an option. The gunman would hear her.

She spotted the parking attendant on the far side of the lot, waving his arms like a maestro, conducting a massive pickup truck as it maneuvered to fit into one of the few remaining spaces.

Rising with shaking knees to a half-bent position, Martha began to back away, intent upon phoning for help, when the harsh voice spoke again. She stopped, terrified the man would hear her movements.

"The keys! I want the keys now!"

Martha reversed course and inched closer to the SUV. She peered through a thin strip of the filthy back window, where a child had scrawled "wash me." The sandy-haired man was holding out his keys. As she watched, he dropped them. However, instead of dropping them straight into the mugger's outstretched hand, the man flicked them sideways. The keys clattered to the ground under the minivan. A look of thrilled delight filled the mugger's face as he raised the gun toward the sandy-haired man's head. His finger began to slowly squeeze the trigger.

Screaming, Martha straightened up and launched her purse at the gunman. The mugger's eyes flew to Martha as her ten-pound purse crashed into his stomach. The sandy-haired man pounced for the gun.

A loud bang reverberated between the vehicles as Martha jumped back behind the SUV and covered her face with her hands. The echo died, allowing the rumble of city traffic to reassert itself. Martha uncovered her face and hunched down to peer under the vehicle. The sandy-haired man lay sprawled on the asphalt, motionless and bleeding. The mugger's feet were gone.

A second later, the parking attendant reached her side. "Call 911!" she called, as she rushed to the bleeding man. The attendant pulled out a cell phone and began to dial.

Martha ripped off her lightweight cotton sweater and balled it up in her hands. A small hole under the man's right collar-bone oozed blood, but a puddle of blood was forming under him. Pushing him on his side, Martha could see the man's entire back was drenched with dark blood pouring from the gaping exit wound near his shoulder blade. Cramming her balled-up sweater over the hole, she tried to staunch the stream of blood. Between the vehicles, the warm, unmoving air was so laden with the iron scent of blood that Martha could taste it.

Gasping in pain, the man's eyes fluttered open and he groaned. He tried to push Martha away and twisted his legs under him to try to stand.

"Don't move! Help is coming! We'll get you to the hospital," Martha said, praying under her breath that the ambulance would hurry. The blood was beginning to soak through her sweater onto her hands.

The parking attendant, a slight, dark-skinned Indian man, knelt by her side. "I called 911. Help should be here any second. The station is not far," he said in mildly accented British English.

Sirens sounded in the distance.

The man on the ground spoke, but his words were lost in the background noise.

"What did you say?" Martha leaned over him, putting her ear close to his mouth.

"My baby. Van is hot."

"He says he doesn't want the baby to get hot in the van. Can you see if there's a baby? I can't take the pressure off."

The attendant jumped to his feet and ran around the van. Martha heard him pull the side door open and call out, "Yes, the baby is in a car seat," before the sirens drowned out whatever else he said.

Paramedics appeared at Martha's side. As they took over, Martha scooted back out of the way and bumped into the feet of a police officer, who offered her a hand to help her up. Mechanically wiping the blood from her hands onto her slacks, Martha watched the paramedics work.

"Are you injured, Ma'am?" the police officer asked.

"No, I saw what happened. This is his blood, not mine."

The memories stopped there, and Martha glanced at her green dress, splotched with raindrops, instead of blood.

The shooter's face was imprinted on her brain. She'd spent over an hour describing him to a sketch artist for the police. The resulting picture was jolting in its accuracy. She could see his dark eyes; black, spiky hair; and stubbly, brown face, which was round with flat cheeks and a long nose that hooked at the end. He looked maybe Latino or Native American. She even remembered his clothes, which seemed odd, since it felt like she'd mostly focused on the gun in his hand. Closing her eyes, Martha pictured the man in her mind. He had worn blue jeans and a gray sport coat over a pale-colored shirt. Maybe light blue? She couldn't remember his shoes.

She looked at her hands. The blood was gone now, but she could remember how it had felt. Her hands had been sticky. Dark, drying blood had been caught in the lines in her palms, in the crevices around her cuticles, and under her fingernails. She'd had to wash them at the police station.

A memory of the metallic smell of blood saturated the air. A wave of intense guilt and anxiety engulfed her body.

You should have gotten help more quickly instead of standing there and watching. You should have done something more.

The thoughts came in quick succession. A part of her brain tried to fight back.

Shake it off. I did all I could.

She shook her head, hoping the motion would help to remove the thoughts crashing through her brain. Nausea hit.

Get a hold of yourself. You will not throw up!

She fought off the nausea with a few deep breaths.

She focused on the words of the detective who had questioned her for four hours after the shooting. He was a huge man, as big as a Dallas Cowboys football player. "Don't blame yourself. You didn't shoot him. You did your best to stop the bleeding. If he lives, it will be because of you," said Detective Monroe.

Being questioned by him had been odd. The giant detective, Monroe, had asked her every conceivable question in an attempt to elicit every tiny detail from her memory. They reviewed the shooting at least four times, each time with slight variations of the same questions. Martha had felt like she was being questioned by an inexplicably gentle, yet ruthlessly persistent, Goliath. At least six and a half feet tall, maybe even closer to seven feet, the detective had given her the impression of a protective tower hovering over her. As they had walked through the police station, he had automatically ducked his head when they had passed through door frames.

Now, it felt as if the shooting had happened in an alternate reality, not this morning on the way to work.

The elevator doors opened. Three nurses rushed by as an alarm went off somewhere. Martha watched them disappear into a room, hoping the patient in trouble wasn't Curt Holliczek.

Chapter 2

Martha turned around and saw a nurse's area with a bank of computer monitors showing the current vital statistics on the different patients. Scrub-wearing people stood working near the computers. One nurse conferred with a doctor. Another nurse checked monitors. A young man was rapidly carrying a stack of IV solutions down the long corridor that stretched to the right and left. A rosacea-faced woman with three chins and a hefty bosom sat entering data into a computer, mechanically flipping through each chart in a pile by her elbow and moving them to form a new pile on the floor by her feet.

"Excuse me. Is it okay to leave this card for Curt Holliczek?" Martha asked.

The clerk glanced up with a perky smile that was at odds with the painful redness of her face. "One minute. Let me check with his nurse."

The heavy woman turned from the computers and called out to a nurse standing by the bank of monitors. "Jenn, can this lady take a card to Mr. Holliczek?"

"He's still sleeping, and he's not supposed to have any visitors, but his wife is with him. If you'd like, I'll ask her to step out here."

"Yes, thank you," Martha said.

The nurse trotted down the hall silently and vanished into a room down the corridor.

Talking to the man's wife in front of the crowd at the desk area would be unfathomable. Martha hated having to speak in front of other people. Her shyness and anxiety around groups of people made her shrink inward into a protective cocoon if she hadn't prepared herself to face them. She was an extreme introvert. Having to face people all day sucked the energy out of her, leaving her tired and in need of a peaceful recharge in the evenings. Like most introverts, she forced herself to deal with the world. Life required it. Martha had a strong sense of empathy and a deeply ingrained, faith-based belief that people should help others. To roll up into a ball and ignore the world would be abandoning her duty. However, she did have mental tricks and methods of handling people on her own terms.

Martha walked down the hall to meet Mrs. Holliczek closer to the room, where they might speak with a bit more privacy.

Jenn reappeared from behind a wide door and pulled it closed behind her.

"Mrs. Holliczek will be right out." She smiled, knocked on the door to the next room, opened it, and vanished again.

The card felt slippery in her sweating hands. Her face flamed red with embarrassment and nerves. Meeting new people was always hard for her, and feeling like she'd failed the woman's husband made this meeting doubly hard. Martha closed her eyes and ordered herself to calm down.

When she opened her eyes, a petite, black-haired, brown-skinned woman was standing in front of her. Mrs. Holliczek's red-rimmed, black eyes held a puzzled look.

"Hello, Mrs. Holliczek. I'm sorry to bother you. I wanted to give your husband this card and wish him well." Martha paused. She wasn't saying what she needed to say. She needed to back up and introduce herself.

"I'm Martha Rowan. I was walking across the parking lot this morning and saw your husband get shot. I'm sorry I couldn't do more to help him." Martha felt tears beginning to form around the edges of her eyes. She blinked them away.

"The police told me that a woman walking by had helped Curt by throwing her purse at the gunman, putting pressure on the wound to stop the bleeding, and asking someone to call an ambulance. Was that you?" Her gentle voice flowed with a soft staccato accent that suggested either foreign parentage or foreign birth. An orange, embroidered blouse gave her brown skin a warm glow. Well-fitting jeans flattered her round hips. Bright orange toenails popped out of unseen sandals, which were hidden by the bottom of her jeans.

"Yes," Martha answered.

"Thank you so much! You have no reason to be sorry. Curt owes his life to you. You did much more than many people would. Most people are afraid to touch a bleeding person. Curt could have bled to death before the ambulance got there, if you hadn't helped him." She stepped forward and hugged Martha, who stiffened with surprise, since she wasn't one for hugging people she didn't know very well.

"I brought a card for your husband. I put my name and email address inside. If ... when ... if you want to know what I saw, I'll tell you. I know you probably don't want to hear about it now." Martha held out the card.

"Please, call me Alegria. Yes, I absolutely want to hear anything you can tell me. Do you have time now? Curt is sleeping. The doctors gave him something for the pain, and they want him to sleep now."

"Is he ...?" Martha paused, staring at the door to the room, picturing the sandy-haired man, pale, connected to tubes and beeping machines. She pictured him again, lying on the asphalt in a pool of blood. The blood had stained her semi-casual office clothes. The police had collected them into evidence. She hoped she never had to see the knit twin-set and slacks again. She'd had to go home for proper clothing before driving to the hospital since the scrubs that the police had provided her with had been too big. Focusing on Mrs. Holliczek, Martha tried to form a sentence, but didn't know how to ask politely if the woman's husband would survive.

Alegria gave her a smile and patted her arm. "The doctors tell me he will be fine. He has a high risk of infection, but the bullet missed the major arteries. One of his lungs collapsed, and the area where the bullet exited will take time to heal over, but they think he will recover completely."

"Oh, thank God!"

"The nurses have been telling me that I must go eat. Will you join me for coffee in the cafeteria? I didn't feel like going alone. You can tell me what happened," said Alegria.

"If you are sure you want to hear about it, absolutely, I'll come."

Alegria paused as they passed the nurses' station to tell Jenn that she was going to the cafeteria.

Martha wrapped her fingers around a cup of hot chocolate and shivered in the refrigerated air of the cavernous cafeteria. She wished she'd brought the sweater she usually kept in her car for this common summer problem—outdoor temperatures greater than one hundred degrees and indoor temperatures in the mid-sixties. She sipped the cocoa and wished her stomach would stop churning nervously. She hadn't purchased food. She couldn't face eating while telling Mrs. Holliczek what happened. The memory of the blood on the pavement made her queasy.

Explaining what happened didn't take long. Martha wished she knew how the police were progressing in identifying the gunman. "I wish I had ..."

"No, don't you apologize. You saved Curt's life today. The one to blame is the man with the gun. The police will catch him soon since you were able to describe him." Alegria nibbled a crumb-topped blueberry muffin and sipped a cup of coffee.

Martha winced inwardly. She'd come to offer comfort to the victim's wife, but instead the victim's wife was comforting her. She was being a nuisance after all.

Alegria jumped from her seat and raised her hand, her eyes focused on someone behind Martha. Twisting around, Martha saw a man, maybe in his late twenties, neatly dressed in navy slacks with a red-and-blue polo shirt, making his way through the tables toward them. His mouth was pinched in a flat line. His hair, which grew in dark, thick waves, was darker than Curt's, and his features were more handsome, but Martha could see a family resemblance. Martha stood up, but the man didn't notice her. All of his attention was on Alegria, whom he pulled into a quick, strong hug.

"The nurse upstairs told me you were here. How's Curt? What did the doctor say about his surgery?"

"Daniel, he's going to be fine. The surgery went well, but the doctors gave him something for the pain, and they want him to sleep now."

"What happened? Who shot him? Why?"

"I was finding that out myself." Alegria put her arm around Martha's shoulders. "This is Martha. She saved Curt's life this morning. Martha, this is Daniel, Curt's brother."

Martha's cheeks glowed with heat, "Oh! I wish I could have prevented the whole thing. I did what anyone would do after it happened."

Martha forced herself to stop looking at the floor and look at Daniel. She found him staring at her with the most outrageously colored eyes she'd ever seen, an amber color that was a shade darker than pale orange. Their eyes locked; her green clicked in with his amber and wouldn't disengage.

"Thank you for what you did for Curt," he said. "I'd like to hear what happened." He held out a chair for Martha. She managed to sit without missing the chair. The world felt askew.

Alegria gave Daniel a list of Curt's injuries, the treatment he'd received, and the doctor's thoughts on his prognosis and recovery. Martha listened, trying not to stare at Daniel's eyes. She began to feel that she was intruding on a family conversation and should leave them to talk.

You're in the way. You should go. Calm down. They want to talk to you. You will not run away. Relax.

When Alegria finished speaking, Daniel turned to Martha and caught her staring at his eyes again. He smiled, and Martha realized that people probably reacted oddly to the color of his eyes all the time. He was undoubtedly used to it.

"So, tell me. How did Curt get shot?" he said.

Martha described walking into the mugging, hiding, and watching Curt drop the keys. She told how she had thrown her purse as the gunman prepared to shoot, how Curt had grabbed the gun, and how it had gone off. She felt as if she were reciting a speech by rote. Daniel and Alegria wouldn't know how deeply she cared about the events she'd seen. Her words felt flat and unemotional. She didn't have the energy left to give her speech the emotion it deserved. To her horror, tears began to stream down her face.

"Are you okay? You look like you've had it for today," said Daniel.

"Daniel! Of course, she is tired. She's been through a lot," said Alegria. She frowned at Daniel and gave him a look of pure exasperation, like a mother reprimanding her child for the same offense for the hundredth time.

"Please, don't worry about me. I'm tired. That's all." Martha swiped the tears away with the base of her palm. "I had to go over this with the police several times. I guess it took more out of me than I thought."

I need to go home and recharge. Rest. Get away from people for a while.

Alegria pulled tissues from her purse and handed them to Martha. Turning to Daniel, Alegria said, "Curt must have thrown the keys to keep the man from taking little Felix. The man didn't know Felix was in the van. Why would anyone attempt a car-jacking in downtown during morning rush hour?"

"It was risky, even stupid, to try at that time of day. I'm not surprised that Curt grabbed the gun. Given half a chance, I would have done the same," said Daniel. His eyes, now serious and a little concerned, darted to Martha, but landed back on Alegria.

Martha blotted her face and listened to them. Alegria was giving her a chance to pull herself together. Sweet of her.

"Is Felix the baby? Is he okay? He was screaming when the paramedics took him away," said Martha.

"He's fine. He doesn't like strangers very much right now. He's at home with my sister, Veronica," said Alegria.

"Martha, can I give you a ride home? I don't think you're in any shape to drive," said Daniel.

"Daniel!" said Alegria, frowning down his word choice and phrasing again. "Martha, I'm sure you are tired. You've had a traumatic day. Would you let Daniel drive you?"

"Curt had a much worse day than I did. You'll want to be here to see him when he wakes up. I didn't want to add to your worries. I'm fine, only tired. Besides, I wouldn't want to leave my car here," said Martha.

"I could drive you in your car and leave mine here. I'll take a taxi back or have a friend come get me. I do want to see Curt, but I'd rather see him when he's awake, and that won't be for some time yet. Will it, Alegria?"

"The doctor said it would be best if he sleeps for several hours. Please, Martha, let him do this for you," said Alegria, as she reached out and took both of Martha's hands into her own.

"Okay. I shouldn't have come down here. I didn't realize how tired I was."

"We are glad you came, Martha. Thank you for telling us what happened. We are lucky you were near Curt today. You were his guardian angel," said Alegria.

They all stood up from the table. Alegria came around and hugged Martha again.

Martha tried not to stiffen. "You will let me know how Curt is doing, won't you?" she asked.

"Absolutely. I have your number and email here," said Alegria, waving the card Martha had given her.

The storm that chased Martha into the hospital had blown itself out, leaving heat and humidity behind it. Martha led Daniel through the parking lot to her car, avoiding the deeper puddles as she went.

Chapter 3

"Where to?" Daniel asked as he adjusted the driver's seat and mirrors.

"Take I-35 North. I'll let you know where to exit."

Relieved to have someone else driving, Martha melted into her seat. Half her brain wanted to go to sleep. The other half wanted to see how Daniel handled her car. He drove smoothly, with confidence, in the heavy traffic. Rush hour started at four-thirty p.m. in Dallas, and it was almost that time already.

She studied Daniel. His oval face had a strong, rounded chin, a straight nose, and high, well-defined cheekbones. The flat plains of his cheeks would have been entirely pale had he not had such dark facial hair. He'd shaved, but the follicles still gave his face a shadow. His amber eyes were closely set together and extremely alert, tracking the traffic around them. She guessed his age to be a few years more than her own twenty-three years.

Martha almost forgot to tell Daniel where to exit to get to her apartment in Carrollton. In what seemed like no time, she was directing him where to park. He followed her up the sidewalk from the parking area to the door of her apartment.

The buildings in the complex had white limestone façades with gabled windows, creating the appearance of several large houses clustered together instead of apartment buildings. The homes were landscaped with rows of holly bushes and overplanted seasonal flower beds filled with snapdragons. Courtyards of St. Augustine grass between the buildings were shaded with large crape myrtle trees. Well-placed benches invited residents to sit and enjoy the greenery.

Martha fumbled for her keys and for the words to invite Daniel inside her place. She wanted to be alone, but she wanted to be polite even more. "Would you like to come in while you wait for your ride back to the hospital?" she asked as she aimed her key toward the door's deadbolt lock.

Before she could insert the key, the door flew open. Daniel pounced forward and pushed her away from the door as the barrel of a gun appeared in front of her. Martha stumbled back onto the pavement as a black-clothed man in a ski mask materialized in her doorway. He took aim with the gun, targeting Martha. Daniel's hand shot out, knocking the gun upward, and grabbed the man's arm to flip him over. The gunman went tumbling to the ground. Martha darted into the holly bushes lining the sidewalk to keep from being crushed. The man rolled like a ball and came to his feet as deftly as an acrobat.

Daniel jabbed his right fist and blood exploded from the intruder's mouth. Daniel moved to strike again, but the man sidestepped, spun, and kicked out, planting his foot into Daniel's abdomen. Daniel grunted as the air was knocked out of him. He fell back, fighting for breath.

Martha turned to look for the gun, now lying on the pavement, but the man was faster. He swooped down and scooped up the gun. The man swung around looking for her as Martha dove into her apartment and away from the open door. A bullet buried itself in the door frame.

Daniel surged to his feet and dove again for the gun, but missed as the intruder backpedaled, pivoted on one foot, and ran. He vanished around the corner in the direction of the parking lot.

"Martha! Are you okay?"

"Yeah … yes." She peeked around the doorframe. "Is he gone?"

From the parking lot, sounds of wheels peeling out as a car sped out of the complex reached their ears. Daniel ran to the parking lot and Martha followed, but both were too late to see anything. The car had vanished around the corner of the next building.

"He's gone. I'm calling 911."

"Okay," she said softly, feeling faint as her blood pounded in her ears and the adrenaline coursing through her veins induced a tremor that started in her torso and moved down to her knees. She listened as he gave the cross streets and the name of her apartment complex into the phone. When he was done with the call, she said, "You were incredible! How did you know he was there? You pushed me back before I even knew something was wrong." The whole episode felt unreal. Disjointed images flew through Martha's memory like a movie she had watched, not like an event in which she'd participated.

"I have reflexes honed by the threat of IEDs. It kept me alive in Iraq." He grinned at her, his even, white front teeth showing, and her heart tripped over itself. His amber eyes were alight.

Within a minute, sirens sounded, and a police car pulled into the complex.

"Wow, they were fast," said Daniel. He walked over to meet the officers as they emerged from their patrol car.

"How did you get here so quickly?" asked Daniel.

"Dispatch received three calls about a man dressed in black with a gun trying to shoot two people. We were in the area. Are you the two people who were attacked?" asked the officer.

Two hours later, Martha and Daniel stood outside the Carrollton Police Department and Judicial Complex off Jackson Road. The officer in charge, Lieutenant Silk, a thirty-ish, blonde, Louisiana native with a syrupy drawl, had finished questioning them. Lieutenant Silk had been every bit as thorough as Detective Monroe, but without the towering, powerful bulk. Instead, he was five feet and ten inches of soft-bodied, young male, smooth-faced and relaxed. While healthy in his appearance, he lacked the musculature of even a weekend athlete.

Lieutenant Silk had thanked them both for their cooperation, promised to get back in touch with them soon, and released them for the evening.

"You can't go home. Do you have a place to stay?" Daniel asked as they stood together on the sidewalk in the shade of the building.

"I'm going to a hotel for the night. I'll call someone to ask for a place to stay tomorrow," Martha said with more confidence than she felt. Finding somewhere to stay would be a challenge.

Sure, you can pick up the phone and call someone. If you knew anyone to call. If you were capable of making a phone call at all. STOP! I'll figure that out later.

Daniel's expression was watchful. "I don't know what's going on or why Curt was attacked. But it looks like somebody doesn't want to leave any witnesses. It can't be a coincidence that a masked gunman attacked you on the same day that you witnessed my brother being shot. What I can't figure out is how that guy knew where you lived." The worry lines between Daniel's eyebrows were deep, and the amber eyes somber. "Are you sure you'll be okay at a hotel? Do you have any friends you can stay with?"

The three months she'd been in Dallas hadn't been long enough for someone as shy as she was to have made any friends. Martha ignored that question. "Could the shooter have followed me when I left downtown and came home? He would've had to watch for me to leave the police station.

He must have had nerves of steel to stay that close while the police were looking for him."

"Maybe. Or maybe he has an accomplice, and someone else watched for you. We don't even know if the guy who shot at us was the same guy who attacked Curt. He got smart and wore a mask this time."

"I had an idea about that. Maybe he didn't wear a mask downtown because that would have been too conspicuous, even from a distance. From across the street, the gun would have been hard to see, since he held it close to him. To the casual observer, he and Curt would look like two guys talking between the cars. I had to practically walk into them to know what was going on." Martha looked at her car, wondering if she should say goodbye or offer Daniel a ride.

"I called Alegria while you were still talking to the police and let her know what happened. She said Curt woke up briefly, but is sleeping again. I told her I was going to stop and get some dinner. Do you want to join me?"

At the mention of food, Martha realized that she hadn't had anything to eat since breakfast except for the cup of hot chocolate she'd had at the hospital. She'd neglected to eat lunch in her rush to get to the hospital to find out if Curt had survived and hadn't felt like eating in her anxiety about talking to Alegria. Between the incident that morning and the attack at her apartment, Martha felt as if she'd run two marathons since breakfast. Now that the adrenaline rush had gone, she felt drained and hollow. She'd need food soon, or she'd be too weak to stand, with a throbbing headache from the hunger.

Don't stand here staring. Answer! You need to eat! At least you won't be alone if someone is still out there watching you. If he means it. Why would he want to eat with you? Who cares why! Answer him!

She tilted her head sideways to move out of the glare off a car windshield, and stared into Daniel's eyes again. "Are you sure? I mean, okay. Where do you want to go?"

"I know a Columbian place not far from here. Have you ever had Columbian food?"

"No. Is it spicy?"

"Not hot spicy, for the most part. More garlic, onions, and herbs." He smiled, and Martha watched the light go on in his eyes. The amber almost flickered.

"Okay. I'm willing to try. Give me directions and I'll drive."

They left the Judicial Complex and turned south on Josey Lane. In less than ten minutes, they arrived at a hole-in-the-wall restaurant in an outdated shopping center. The parking lot was full of potholes holding dirty brown water from the earlier rain. In spite of the rundown appearance of the lot, the businesses nearby were a thriving ethnic mix. A Chinese supermarket abutted a Latino music store. Greek and Vietnamese restaurants nearby were packed with a dinner rush. A Mexican meat market did brisk business.

Daniel held the door and ushered Martha into the dimly lit restaurant decorated with South American flags and a variety of handmade knick-knacks covering the walls. A hostess led them to a small booth with a lit candle on the table. Martha took in her surroundings, from the giant television hanging in front of the windows, which someone had tuned to a soccer game, to the homey craft works and paintings of mountains and peasants on the wall opposite her. The place was proudly South American, and intimate and cozy in its atmosphere. Martha was glad for the low lights. They hid the dirt smudges on her green denim dress and the scratches on her arms from her tumble into the bushes. She didn't care about trendy clothes, but she did have her own classic style and a preference for a tidy appearance.

The waitress took their drink orders. Martha requested iced tea, but Daniel ordered something Martha had never heard of and couldn't pronounce.

"What did you order to drink? I didn't understand," she said.

"I ordered a *batido de maracuya con leche*, a fruit smoothie with a milk base."

"What kind of fruit?"

"In English it's called passion fruit. It's from Brazil. I get it every time I come in here."

"You eat here often, then?" Martha looked around at the restaurant again to keep from staring at him. The candlelight was dancing in his eyes, making them glow like warm orange honey.

"I come here with Alegria and Curt every couple of months. It's Alegria's favorite place to eat. She's originally from Peru. She says the foods in Columbia, Ecuador, Peru, and Venezuela are virtually identical, with only minor differences. We come here when she wants a taste of home."

After looking over the menu and letting Daniel explain a few of the listings to her, Martha and Daniel ordered. He selected a *bandeja paisa*, a sampler platter with a variety of food, while Martha ordered an *empanada* plate containing half-moon-shaped pastries full of flavorful meat and vegetables with a side salad and rice. Both dishes came with *plátanos maduros*, which Daniel explained were plantains, which were similar to bananas, cooked in oil after they ripened completely, so they were *maduro*, or mature, as opposed to green, which cooked differently.

"Is Curt your only sibling?" Martha asked, looking for a way to keep the conversation moving. She didn't mind silence, but she knew most people considered conversing to be more polite.

"No, we have a younger sister. She's a college student down at UT Austin." Daniel ran a hand through his thick hair, rumpling the dark waves. The worried look Martha had seen at the hospital returned to his face and his eyes dimmed, focusing somewhere inside his head.

"Curt will be fine, won't he? The doctors said he would recover fully, didn't they?" she asked, still watching his eyes.

Daniel's eyes lit up again. "Yes, he's internally hardwired with mental resilience and a drive to get his own way, which is a polite way of saying he's stubborn. He'll be fine, and he'll have a great scar to show for it. He'll like that. We used to compare scars when we were teenagers. We almost had a competition going to see who had the most stitches."

"Who won?"

"Until today, I was ahead. I crashed through a plate-glass door when I was learning to rollerblade."

A waitress appeared with their plates balanced on her arm. Conversation stopped as both got busy with their meals. Martha ate hungrily. She felt as if she hadn't eaten all day. The food was good. The empanadas were tasty. The plantains were soft and stickily sweet. Martha wasn't sure she liked them at first, but the taste grew on her. Before she finished, she decided that she'd have to come back to the restaurant again. When they'd finished half their plates, Daniel resumed the conversation.

"What do you do downtown?" he asked.

"I'm a worker's compensation claims handler for a commercial real estate developer. When people get hurt on building projects, I process the paperwork to get the bills for the medical care paid. How about you? What do you do?"

"During the week, I'm the software and IT department for a twenty-five-person consulting company up in Plano. I'm also still in the Army Reserve. So, I spend some weekends and a week here and there training."

"You mentioned having a sixth sense for explosive devices. Your unit was called up, then. Did you go to Iraq and Afghanistan?"

"Both, once each for a total of 24 months."

Martha looked up from her plate. Daniel was looking down at his plate. She couldn't tell if the subject was one she should ask about or avoid. Her curiosity won. "When were you there?"

"I was in Iraq for 2009 and Afghanistan for 2012. Curt deployed to Iraq twice. He was active-duty Army before he married Alegria."

"Does the military run in your family?"

"Yes, my dad served in the Army, and my grandfather was a Marine. We've got old black-and-white photos of men in uniform going back generations on my mother's side."

They lapsed into silence as Martha pondered how much she should ask about Daniel's military experiences. She didn't want to be nosy. She had decided to save the subject for another time and ask something else when Daniel spoke.

"Afghanistan was rough. I had a few truly bad days. Curt saw more action than I did." He smiled at Martha and her eyes locked on his. That smile and those eyes were such a smooth combination; she thought Daniel had to know exactly what kind of effect he was having. He could turn the charm on and off with ease.

He laughed suddenly, and Martha blushed, wondering if he could possibly read her mind. She erased the thought and reached for her iced tea, breaking their eye contact like breaking a seal on a jar. She imagined a suction "pop" when she finally managed to drag her eyes away.

They'd both emptied their plates. The waitress reappeared to ask if they wanted any dessert.

"The *tres leches* is delicious here. Do you want some?" said Daniel.

"No, I'm full. Thanks."

Daniel asked for the bill, and they sat for a moment, comfortably silent, finishing their drinks, until the waitress returned and handed the bill to Daniel.

"Can we split it?" Martha asked.

"I invited you. I've got it." He handed the waitress the bill and a credit card.

A few moments later, Daniel held the heavy glass door to the restaurant open and followed Martha out into the soft pink light of sunset. Daniel glanced inside her car, obviously scanning for trouble before he opened the driver's door for Martha. Martha leaned against the warm metal of the car door frame. Heat radiated from the cooling asphalt, warming the thin soles of her sandals.

"I don't want to scare you, but please be careful. Whoever this guy is, he'll probably try again," said Daniel.

"I know. Thank you. You saved my life today."

Daniel's eyebrows shot up in mock surprise, the amber eyes open wide. "Then we're even, since you saved Curt." He leaned forward, grasped Martha by the shoulders and lightly brushed her cheek with a kiss. "Goodnight. I need to get back to the hospital to see Curt. Alegria probably thinks I fell off the face of the earth."

"How are you getting back to the hospital? Do you want me to take you? I'm perfectly awake now." A warm breeze blew the fine wisps of hair at her temples into her face, where they clung to the shimmering layer of dampness covering her skin. The evening air was a sauna.

"I'll call a friend who lives nearby. He should be here in a few minutes. If he can't come, I'll get a taxi. Besides, I was taking you home. Don't worry about me," Daniel said. "Go to a hotel. Get some sleep." He stepped back, away from the car, and pulled out his phone.

Martha got into her car and waved goodbye as she started the engine. She watched Daniel as she pulled out of the parking space.

The words "be careful" echoed in Martha's head, almost as if Daniel was sitting next to her saying them again. Martha looked up to see Daniel in her rearview mirror. He was on the phone. It was his voice she had heard, not her own usual inner monologue. Martha chalked it up to exhaustion and tension. Her memory was replaying his warning.

Driving east on Beltline Road, Martha arrived in the city of Addison's restaurant row in a matter of minutes. Hotels from every chain in the state were interspersed with the restaurants. Choosing one at random, Martha pulled into a parking lot and checked into a room for the night.

"OUCH!" MARTHA WINCED as she dabbed a warm, damp washcloth on the scrapes on her elbows and arms. One nasty, raw spot ached. She recalled inflicting the wound when she fell to the sidewalk at her apartment. The gleaming bathroom's wide mirror highlighted the many scratches and cuts on her arms. Martha's long-standing hatred of holly bushes grew. She'd never encountered them without coming away worse off from the meeting. Vowing never to plant a holly bush when she got a home of her own, Martha finished her ministrations and forced herself to focus on more pressing matters.

The hotel was fine for a night, but it was anonymous and impersonal. Martha felt isolated. She wanted to be in a place with other people, people who would give her advice or come to her rescue if needed. She paced the floor between the bed and the short dresser that passed for a television stand. The question was, who could give her a place to stay?

Martha picked up her phone and stared at it. She desperately wanted to call someone and talk about what had happened, but she had no one to call. Her parents were on a month-long cruise celebrating their thirtieth anniversary. No way was she going to panic them while they were so far away, especially since her mother had been so worried about her moving 250 miles away from home.

She considered calling Lorena, but rejected the idea. A glance at the clock showed it was 7:30pm. That meant it was the middle of the night in Rome, where Lorena was. Lorena had been her best friend through high school. They'd gone to the University of Texas and roomed together for four years. During the last year, Lorena's younger sister had lived with them, too. Lorena was the sister Martha had never had. However, Lorena had opted to do graduate studies in Rome. She'd packed up and left for Europe at the same time Martha had left for Dallas. Lorena would freak out if Martha left her a message saying she'd seen a man shot. She couldn't do that to Lorena. It wouldn't be fair.

Making phone calls to people she didn't know very well was difficult. Since moving to the Dallas area three months ago, Martha hadn't made any friends. However, that wasn't surprising since she sometimes took years to decide to call someone a friend. In her mind, most people were categorized as acquaintances.

She had a system for meeting people. She wasn't a recluse, only shy. Making friends in town was definitely something she had planned to do. She simply hadn't had time to accomplish it yet. Since she was so shy that dealing with people was hard for her, she had tried to approach the problem logically. For her, making friends involved time and contact and joining organizations.

First, Martha joined a church, because she always felt at home at church. She had been raised by religious parents and considered herself to be strongly religious. Logically, meeting people with similar beliefs could lead to friendships eventually. She'd scanned the social groups available at the church and had gone to three monthly meetings of the singles' group in an effort to start meeting people. Next, she'd found a local adult recreational volleyball league and joined that. She'd needed the exercise, enjoyed the sport, and, again, would have a chance to meet the same people regularly. However, the practices and games hadn't started yet, so she hadn't met anyone through volleyball yet. She'd intended to volunteer someplace, maybe an animal shelter or library, since she had been raised with a strong sense of volunteerism and she enjoyed the feeling of contributing to the community. Martha's mother had been the queen of volunteer organizations. However, she hadn't found a place to volunteer yet.

Reviewing her options, Martha realized her only choices were the people she'd met at the church singles group. Those people at the meetings had been friendly. The best course of action would be to call one of them. She could meet someone for lunch, explain the situation, and maybe stay at the new friend's place the next night. The only problem was that her shyness made calling someone she didn't know well difficult.

Why can't I do this? Why can't I make a stupid phone call? All I have to do is dial and say, "Hi, would you like to go to lunch with me tomorrow or the next day?" This is beyond introverted. This is ridiculous. You need therapy. Come on. Dial.

Martha sat on the mauve-draped bed, phone in hand. She reviewed the people she'd met at church and decided to call a young woman named Allie. They had chatted well together. Allie had been outgoing, easy to talk to. They'd both attended private, religious schools as children. Even better, both worked in downtown Dallas.

Besides, what's the worst that could happen? She could say she's too busy for lunch. Big deal. Come on. DIAL!

Chapter 4

Martha dialed the phone and it began to ring.

"Hello?"

"Hello, is this Allie?"

"Yes."

"Hi, this is Martha Rowan. We met at St. Mary's?"

"Oh, hi. How are you?"

"I'm fine. I was wondering if you were free for lunch tomorrow or the next day? Or, if not for lunch, are you free for dessert tomorrow night?" Martha could feel the anxiety kicking into her stomach, her nerves tightening, her face going red, and sweat forming on her scalp.

You're talking too much. Shut up.

Allie didn't answer.

"Are you there?"

"Yes, it's ... I'm sorry. I always eat lunch at my desk. Work has been so busy that I don't get out at all during the day. I've got some family issues that are taking up a lot of my free time right now. What little social time I've got is pretty well scheduled. I'm blessed with more friends and family than I have time to see right now," Allie said.

Martha went numb. She cleared her throat and fought to keep her voice from cracking. "Oh, I see. That's okay. I understand. I'll see you at church. Have a pleasant evening. Goodbye."

"Goodbye."

The room spun slightly, and Martha slumped over on the bed. The phone dangled over the edge of the bed for a second before falling to the floor.

What happened?

She said she didn't have time for any more friends. You idiot. Saying "no" to lunch wasn't the worst possible outcome. This is the worst possible outcome. She not only rejected lunch, she rejected getting to know you at all, at any time or place, because you are not worth knowing. Not worth her time.

Martha closed her eyes and fought the stream of negative thoughts that began to flow through her brain. Shutting off one flow only opened another as her brained ricocheted from one mistake to the next, homing in on her failure to prevent Curt being shot. He would have been better off if she hadn't been there at all. After a while, she tried to force herself out of her head and back into the present, making herself study the room around her.

The ceiling over the bed was a flat expanse of freshly painted white—no cracks, smudges, or inexplicable shoe prints. Gray, summer-evening light filtered into the room through the sheer layer of curtain covering the window. A traffic light from the street below changed from red to green, the colors reflecting off the television. Martha crawled off the bed and closed the heavier curtain layer. Spying her phone on the floor, she picked it up and turned the power off for the night. The phone needed charging, so she plugged it into the wall. A quick yank removed the lightweight mauve bedspread from the bed. She threw it over the desk chair. The bedside clock read 8:15 p.m.

Thumbing the remote control through the television stations provided no distraction. The books on her tablet were no help, either. After reaching the end of the same page three times, with no idea of what it had said, Martha gave up on reading. She would probably be awake for hours in spite of feeling completely exhausted, but that was nothing unusual. She'd had nights like this regularly for most of her life, typically caused by minor errors, mistakes, or even nothing at all. At least, today, the incidents that had triggered the insomnia merited the reaction. Her brain was abuzz with recriminations, examinations, doubt, and anxiety.

Martha tried the first step for a night like this. Sometimes a stern mental shake with a focus on the positive could break the loop of thoughts flooding through her brain.

I couldn't have prevented the shooting. I did my best. I did more than most people might have. Daniel likes me. Daniel saved my life. It's not my fault that he had to save me. Alegria was sweet. She says I saved her husband. The police said I did well.

Yet you can't even find a place to stay because you're a social moron. You have no friends here. You're stuck in a hotel by yourself.

STOP! Focus!

So I don't have someone to stay with tonight. It's okay. I'll think of something tomorrow. Pay attention to my surroundings, and I'll be fine.

Martha jumped from the bed and double checked the door lock, sliding the extra chain lock into place. She banged her scraped elbow on the night stand as she jumped back onto the bed. It bled lightly. The bleeding stopped when she held a tissue on it, but this restarted Martha's brain.

So much blood. It came right through your sweater and seeped all over your hands. Microscopic amounts are probably still under your fingernails.

A series of scenes came with the thoughts: Martha lying in a pool of her own blood outside her apartment. The killer's eyes on Martha's face. Little Felix crying in the ambulance.

Enough! Think good thoughts. Think of those beautiful amber eyes. He's going to call tomorrow. Get some sleep.

The clock now read 11:15. Martha flexed and relaxed every muscle in her body from her toes to the top of her head in succession. She tried to remain completely still and mentally recited her bedtime prayers. Her mind kept slipping from the words of the prayers to Curt's face, then Alegria's, Daniel's, and, finally, the killer's. Every word she'd uttered all day suddenly felt stupid, inept. Every movement she'd made was magnified and wrong. Curt's injury was her fault. Her thoughts jumped and shifted. Sleep would never come.

Martha refocused on the prayers and finished saying them. Choosing from memory some of her favorite books, she selected a plot she enjoyed and knew well. Sometimes letting the plot run through her head would help her drift into a dream.

It wasn't working. She focused on a television show, but none of the characters would cooperate in her brain, and most of them were from police procedurals, which reminded her of police stations and statements and shootings and guns. Dreams remained far out of reach. After twenty more minutes, Martha gave up, got up, found her tablet computer, and logged on to The Dallas Morning News. Martha read the entire comics section and worked through both crossword puzzles.

One a.m., and the world was calmer. Martha dropped the tablet on the night stand and clicked off the bedside lamp.

The annoying buzz of the hotel alarm clock sounded at six o'clock. Martha was groggy, tired, and vaguely out of sorts without knowing why for a few seconds. Then the previous day's events came flooding back as she remembered why she was in a hotel. She slapped the alarm clock off and sank back down on the bed. Her pounding heart sped up as the gunman's face flashed before her eyes.

She kicked the covers off her legs and slid her bare feet to the floor. Caught up in her morning routine, Martha jumped into a hot shower that quickly fogged over the bathroom mirror. Abrasive thoughts were forced out and simple preparation and planning for the day took over.

Thirty minutes later, Martha grabbed a bagel, a banana, and a powdered donut from the hotel lobby breakfast nook as she walked out the door to her small green Ford Focus. She smiled as she started the engine. It was her car, her first car that she had bought herself. It was only a year old, with 18,000 miles on it—practically new. Driving it gave her a sense of accomplishment. As much as she loved her car, she still hated to drive it downtown. The nearest Park and Ride for the Green Line downtown train was in old Downtown Carrollton. The Addison Transit Center was closer, though not on the train line. An express bus from Addison to downtown would work as well as the train. So Martha opted for an express bus instead of the train. She drove the few blocks to the Addison Transit Center, eating her breakfast at the stop lights as she went.

The Park and Ride System was one of the Metroplex's great amenities. With its options of trains and express buses, Dallas Area Rapid Transit, or DART, could get her downtown in thirty to forty minutes. She would get to work earlier if she drove herself instead of going to the Park and Ride, but that would require fighting traffic on I-35 East, paying for parking, and paying for more gas. The wear and tear to her nerves and car weren't worth the few minutes she could save by driving herself. Besides, her employer reimbursed her half the cost of the monthly DART pass as part of an effort to support usage of public transportation.

On the bus, Martha sat back, sorting out in her mind what to say to her manager. When she arrived at the West Transfer Station, Martha climbed off with all the other downtown workers, as she had from the train the day before. Only today, she walked all the way around the parking lot that lay between her office and the Depot. The summer sun was beating down between the tall metal-and-glass buildings, turning the concrete island of downtown into an oven. The wind felt like a hair dryer blowing on her skin, drying the sweat that instantly formed on her face. Fluffy white cirrus clouds feathered out across the pieces of pale blue sky visible between the buildings.

Martha turned her head and studied the buildings on the opposite side of the street to avoid accidentally glimpsing a certain area of stained pavement; in the process, she almost walked into a light pole.

She arrived at her cubicle and dumped her things into her desk drawer. After logging on to her computer, Martha went looking for her manager to explain where she'd been all day Tuesday. His office was dark, with an abandoned air to it. No papers littered the desk. No drinks sat out. No briefcase lay propped by the chair where it usually was dropped the moment the manager, Bill, arrived at his desk.

Turning back through the aisles of cubicles, Martha went to the receptionist, who knew everything about schedules and missing managers.

"Hi, Karlyn, do you know if Bill's coming in today?"

"He's not going to be here. He has offsite training at the Fort Worth office today, but he'll be back tomorrow."

"Okay. Thanks."

Martha walked back to her desk feeling dejected. She and Bill were the only ones in the building who handled workers' compensation claims, although a few others handled related bills or insurance claims from non-employees. The other people who sat near Martha were busy tapping away at their own projects. Bill had trained Martha when she'd arrived in May. Her conversations with everyone else had been limited to daily greetings and nods as they passed each other in the rows of cubicles. She couldn't make herself walk up to a near stranger and say, "You'll never guess what happened to me yesterday." At least Bill would be back tomorrow.

Work did not go well. The mail, both electronic and actual, in Martha's inboxes grew exponentially. Files piled up without resolutions. Calculations of payments were error-ridden and had to be corrected and re-entered into the computer. Finally, the computer froze, and she had to reboot.

At noon, Martha popped across the street to a sandwich shop, ate hurriedly, and returned to the office with her heart in her throat. She kept imagining that the shooter was there, downtown, spying from around a corner, or watching her from behind one of the innumerable windows of the shimmering skyscrapers.

The afternoon progressed no better than the morning had. Martha surrendered to the tide of work that threatened to drown her and left for the day at five o'clock having accomplished nothing.

She saw the bus coming as she raced for the stop, and barely made it in time to board before the door closed. As she was taking her seat, she noticed a chubby, dark-haired man running behind the bus. He hadn't made it. The bus pulled away from the curb before he reached the back of it. She felt sorry for him, unlucky soul. He'd have to wait twenty minutes for the next bus.

The trip from the Park and Ride to the hotel was short, but heavy on traffic. Beltline was always busy at rush hour. Martha rejected driving to get dinner without consideration. She hated all that traffic. Luckily, the hotel was in Addison's restaurant row. An independent Italian restaurant, a Tex-Mex chain, and an old-fashioned, Southern home-cooking joint shared the parking lot with the hotel.

Choosing Tex-Mex, Martha walked in for sour cream-topped chicken enchiladas with a chips-and-salsa appetizer and a thirty-two-ounce glass of iced tea. Music in the restaurant was loud, forcing conversation at the tables to be even louder. Noise clogged Martha's head and made her long for the silence of her room. Garish green, red, orange, and yellow colors of serapes, sombreros, and piñatas covering the walls and ceilings didn't have their usual festive feel. Though it had never bothered her before, Martha felt annoyed by the stereotypical cheesiness of the décor. The idea of lingering over her food or drink in the noisy crowd gave her a feeling of claustrophobia. She ate at a tiny table for two in a corner as quickly as she could, then left for the quiet of the hotel.

For the rest of the evening, Martha stared at her phone, willing it to ring with a call from Alegria or Daniel, but it didn't. She kicked herself for not having requested Alegria's phone number. Daniel hadn't offered his, and she hadn't thought to request it. She'd been so sure he would call.

Insomnia and nightmares marked her night at the hotel. Twice she imagined people searching the halls of the hotel, going room to room looking for her. Every footstep past her door caused her heart to race and her stomach to lurch. She set out for work, via the Park and Ride, exhausted but relieved by the fact that Bill would be back today. She almost ran through downtown, blowing past slower pedestrians on the way to her building. She couldn't shake the horrible feeling that someone was watching her.

The elevator in her building was empty as she went up the tower to her floor. The receptionist, Karlyn, called "Good morning" at her as she walked back to her cubicle. Martha managed a hasty nod at her. Reaching her desk, Martha set down her work bag and turned to find her manager, dressed in his usual dark-gray suit slacks and light-blue, button-down shirt with a plaid blue-and-gray tie, coming down the aisle toward her.

"Hi, Martha," Bill Gelise said. "What happened Tuesday? Your message said you had to file a police report. I hope you weren't mugged." Bill looked her over as if checking her for any injury and frowned, spotting the scratches and scrapes on her arms.

Bill was a solid people person who managed the different personalities at the office well and liked to help his employees keep their work and home lives in balance. He was concerned for everyone's wellbeing, operating on the theory that a content worker did a better job than a stressed-out worker. At age fifty-five with graying hair at his temples and a lack of hair on the top of his head, he was a well of information with great problem-solving skills. He was in charge of Martha, helping her handle claims, and supervised several other workers who processed medical bills and other insurance claims.

Martha couldn't help smiling at his concern for her. "I wasn't mugged. I was crossing that parking lot down the street when I walked right into a robbery. I saw a man robbing another man at gunpoint. When the robber raised his gun to shoot, I threw my purse at him. The victim tried to grab the gun and got shot. The gunman ran away. I tried to stop the bleeding until the ambulance arrived. Then, I spent the rest of the morning at the police station filling out witness statements and answering questions. By the time I left, it was after lunchtime, and I still felt like I was covered with blood, so I decided to go home."

"Wow! Did the victim survive, do you know?"

"Yes, he did. I went to the hospital later that day and met his family. His name is Curt Holliczek. His wife said he would be okay." Martha slipped down into her desk chair.

"Are you sure you're okay?" asked Bill, eyeing the scratches on her arms.

"I'm fine. These scratches came later. The victim's brother, his name is Daniel Holliczek, drove me home from the hospital. When we got to my front door, a man jumped out of my apartment with a gun and tried to shoot me. Daniel fought off the man. I'd be dead if Daniel hadn't offered to drive me home. Then, I had to deal with the police again. I couldn't stay at my place, so I've spent the last two nights in a hotel."

"What the hell?! The robber came after you? I mean, it was related to the earlier incident, wasn't it? Two gunmen in one day have to be connected. Why would he come after you? How would he know where you lived?"

"I don't know. Maybe the gunman didn't want to leave a witness. I don't even know that it was the same guy, because the second man was wearing a mask, and the first one wasn't. As for how he found my house, maybe he followed me home?"

"You need to stay somewhere safe with good security. A hotel isn't good enough. Do you want to come and stay at my place? You can have Dora's room. She hasn't used it, except for at Christmas break, since she left for college last year. She's attending a summer session at Texas Tech right now, trying to get some basic courses out of the way so she can get the classes she wants in the fall. My wife won't mind if you use the room. You could ride to work with me." Bill's mouth pinched shut as he watched Martha, waiting for her answer.

Martha looked up at him, barely able to contain the relief flowing through her. She would have a place to stay after all. "Thank you so much! If your wife won't mind, I would appreciate it. I'd like to have people around me."

"I can't believe that guy tried to commit a robbery in broad daylight in the middle of a parking lot. That's brazen to the point of stupidity." Bill squinted as he thought.

"They were standing between two large vehicles, so no one noticed, even with so many people arriving downtown for the morning. I almost walked into them before I knew what was going on. The gunshot wasn't as loud as I'd have expected, either."

Bill was still staring at her with that appraising look in his eye.

"Are you sure you don't need time off?"

"I'd rather work. If I stayed at the hotel all day, I'd go crazy picturing the whole thing again and worrying about the gunman finding me."

"Okay. Well, you're safe here in the office surrounded by people. Nobody is going to march in here and shoot you." Bill rubbed his hands together in a way that made Martha wonder whether he wanted to see someone try to get at her in his office. Then, he switched gears to work mode, straightened his shoulders, and said, "We've got the monthly status meeting this morning, starting in …," he glanced at his watch, "ten minutes, followed by one of those mandatory, all-employees training seminars that HR likes to throw at us. You should have plenty of time to rest. However, I'm afraid the meetings won't challenge the intellect."

Three and a half hours later, Martha emerged hungry from her meetings. Her favorite Chinese food restaurant in the Pedestrian Tunnel Network beckoned. The tunnel network had been dying slowly, disliked and discouraged by city leadership who wanted to move pedestrian traffic out of the tunnels and up to street-level shops. The streets of Dallas frequently appeared empty during the day. However, if people had a choice between walking in the heat radiating off the glass, steel, and concrete of downtown and walking in the air-conditioned tunnels, they'd choose the tunnels.

Radiated heat was a huge problem for the city. The Nasher Sculpture Garden in the Arts District had even had a legal battle with the owner of a neighboring skyscraper after reflected light from its glass became so bright during the construction of the building that exhibitions had to be moved to prevent them from being damaged by the increased heat. To help cool the downtown area and add recreational areas in hopes of enticing people to live downtown, the city built the almost two-acre Belo Garden over what had been a parking lot across from the Cabell Federal Building, and another five-acre park on a deck over a stretch of the Woodall Rogers Freeway. In spite of these efforts, Dallas was still an oven on a summer day.

Sometimes, if she ate a quick lunch at her desk, Martha would use the tunnels to go for a walk, making her way over to the spiral-topped chapel in Thanks-Giving Square and back to her office again. Getting lost in the tunnels was a concern, but she had a good sense of direction and a knack for retracing her steps. In her three months here, she'd come to enjoy the lunchtime challenge of navigating the tunnels.

Martha decided against any walking for the time being, though, remembering she was supposed to be cautious when out by herself.

Bill found Martha on her way out the door to the elevator. "Do you want company?"

"No. I'm tired. I wouldn't be very good company for you. I'm going to eat and read my book," she said, waving her tablet at him.

Her combination fried rice consumed, Martha reached to get her tablet from her purse to read while she finished her iced tea. As she turned to place her purse back on the floor by her chair, her spine stiffened and a wave of fear pulsed through her. Out of the corner of her eye, Martha saw a man watching her. Forcing herself to sit up straight again, Martha turned and looked, convinced that she was overreacting, jittery after all of Tuesday's madness.

She hadn't overreacted. The man who had shot Curt Holliczek was standing a hundred feet away, staring at her from just outside the entry to the restaurant. The look on his face moved from shock to anger. He had come out of the tunnel listening to another dark-haired man who was turned sideways to Martha. The second man was still talking rapidly and didn't seem to realize that his companion had stopped upon recognizing Martha. As Martha watched, the gunman said something to the second man. The second man turned and ran his eyes searchingly through the crowd in the restaurant before identifying Martha. Then, the two men turned and ran, vanishing into the lunchtime-crowded tunnels.

Chapter 5

Stunned, Martha fumbled for her purse and the card that Detective Monroe had given her. She dialed the number on her phone with shaking fingers and a heart pumping with adrenalin.

"Hello, Detective Monroe? This is Martha Rowan. I saw the man who shot Curt Holliczek in the pedestrian tunnels near the Beijing City Restaurant. He's walking with another man."

"Is he still there?"

"No, he went into the tunnels with a crowd of other people, and I can't see him now."

"Where are you?"

"I'm sitting inside the restaurant. I was having lunch."

"Stay there. An officer will be there shortly."

Three minutes later, two uniformed officers appeared at the restaurant's entrance. Martha approached them and identified herself. While she was explaining, the football-player-sized form of Detective Monroe came through the door.

"Are you certain the man you saw was the shooter?" he asked. The uniformed officers moved back deferentially.

"Yes! He was wearing different clothes, but it was the same man. The way he stood and glared at me was exactly how he stood yesterday holding the gun on Mr. Holliczek."

"Which way was he going?"

Martha pointed down the tunnels, toward a flower shop and a dry cleaner where the tunnel curved.

"What was he wearing?"

"A dark-blue, button-down shirt with a light jacket of some kind. I don't know what his pants looked like." Martha closed her eyes, but couldn't bring any more than the man's head and shoulders into focus in her memory. She'd seen him standing there, and knew that his stance was familiar, but the details wouldn't come.

Come on! Focus!

"I'm sorry. I'm not a very good witness today."

"You said he was with someone else. What did he look like?"

"I didn't see anything but his profile. He wasn't facing me. He was turned, talking to the gunman. I was so focused on the man who shot Mr. Holliczek that I didn't look at him. All I can remember is that he was chubby." Martha could feel her face going red.

"That's okay. Give me one moment. I'll be right back." Detective Monroe walked over and spoke to the two uniformed officers. The detective finished speaking to his men, who walked swiftly toward the tunnels. Then, Detective Monroe returned to Martha's side.

"Let me walk you back to your office." He put one arm out in a gesture that clearly meant, "After you." Martha began to walk.

"Won't you search for him?"

"The officers are going to get surveillance footage from the businesses in that stretch of tunnel, and then canvas the area with the sketch to see if anyone recognizes our shooter. I'm going to review the video, looking for him. I'll call you to view the video if I find anyone matching the shooter's description to have you identify him for us. It might take an hour or two to collect and review the video. Having video of him should make him easier to identify. As it turns out, I was going to call you today anyway."

"Why?" Martha asked.

"I got the preliminary report from my counterpart at the Carrollton Police Department regarding the attack at your apartment. Their crime scene unit collected blood from the suspect found at the scene. DNA analysis will give us a name for our suspect if he's in the system for any other crimes. That might take a few weeks to process, though. Meanwhile, please don't walk around downtown alone. I understand you're staying in a hotel. Be careful going from work to the hotel. Try to notice whether someone might be following you. Vary your route home. This man found your home in one afternoon. He may try to follow you to your hotel."

"I will try to be careful. I'm not going to stay at the hotel, though. My manager offered to let me stay with him and his wife for a few days."

"Okay. Let me know the address and contact information for where you'll be."

"I will. Thank you. If I see the man again, what should I do?" asked Martha, coming to a stop outside her building lobby.

"Do what you did. Call me and stay in a crowded area." Detective Monroe looked around at the building lobby entrance. "Is this your building?" Monroe stood tall and shifted his weight to one hip, in a way that reminded Martha of John Wayne in the Saturday night movies she'd watched with her father when she was a child. Her father had the entire John Wayne movie collection.

"Yes. This is it. You'll call about the video?"

"Yes. Goodbye, and be aware of your surroundings."

Martha put her hand up in a quick wave, and then pushed her way through the glass doors into the granite-floored lobby with its bronze-colored elevators.

AN HOUR LATER, Martha sat at her desk, motionless. The computer monitor showed iridescent bubbles floating across an open email window with only the subject line filled. Though her hands were resting on the keyboard, Martha hadn't pressed a key for several minutes. Soon the bubbles would stop, and the screen would go dark.

"Oh!" Martha half yelled as a hand reached out and touched her shoulder.

"Sorry," said Bill. "You weren't responding to my instant messages, so I came over to check on you." He scrutinized her face as he spoke. "What's up? You're even more upset than you were this morning."

"I saw the gunman while I was at lunch. He was talking to another man in the tunnels near that Chinese restaurant I like." She paused for a breath, and then the words tumbled out like a falling pile of blocks, ending in a jumble. "I called the police, and he went away, but the police are checking videos. He's going to call me, and then I have to try to identify him."

"Whoa, *what* now?"

"Sorry, I'm rattled. I saw the gunman while I was at lunch. He and another man were talking in the pedestrian tunnels. He saw me, and he knew I saw him. The gunman and his friend left, and I called the police. The detective on the case, Detective Monroe, sent officers to collect surveillance videos from that area of the tunnels. He's going to call once they review the videos. Then I need to go to the police station to identify the man on video, if he's on there."

"Do you think that the man was looking for you? Could he have followed you?" asked Bill.

"I don't think so. He seemed as surprised to see me as I was to see him. Both men left when they saw me."

The trilling of Martha's desk phone interrupted Bill before he could respond. He nodded for Martha to answer the phone. Martha snatched up the receiver.

"Martha Rowan, how may I help you?"

"Hello, Ms. Rowan. This is Detective Monroe. We'd like you to look at some people on the video for us."

"Hello, Detective. Do you want me to come right now?"

Bill tapped her on the shoulder and mouthed, "I'll drive you."

Martha nodded as Detective Monroe said, "Yes, if you can."

"Okay, I have a ride over. I'll be there shortly. Bye." She replaced the receiver as the detective said goodbye. She grabbed her purse and nodded to Bill. "I'm ready if you are."

Ten minutes later, as Bill slowed to pull into a parking spot near the police station, Martha noticed two familiar faces driving away.

"That was the victim's brother and wife." Martha twisted in her seat to watch them go.

"Where?"

"In the car that was leaving as we were parking. I'll bet the police also asked them to come see if they recognized anyone in the video."

An officer escorted Martha and Bill to a small room to await Detective Monroe. After twenty minutes of tapping her feet, Martha got up and looked around through the department's interior windows to see if she could spot the detective. Not finding him, she sat and resumed her foot-tapping.

Bill watched her. "Martha," he said at last, "please, relax. Given the circumstances, I'd be impatient, too. I can feel the stress building in you. It's like being in a room with a bottle rocket about to go off. I hope they resolve this thing before you hit a breaking point. You're new in town. Do you have any friends or family here? Anyone to talk to about all this?"

Martha stopped tapping her foot and gave him a startled glance. "I'm stressed out right now, but don't worry about me. I can handle it. I'll try to relax. I don't need to talk about it." She took a deep breath and released it slowly.

You already told him what happened. What more is there to say? He's offered a place to stay. You won't be alone. He doesn't need to hear about insomnia or anxiety that you've had your entire life, well before this whole mess started. He doesn't need to know that the shooting replays in your head or that you're completely paranoid because you think people are following you. Do you want your new boss to think you're crazy?

"Do you have any family or friends here in town?" he repeated.

Concern was etched into the wrinkles on Bill's face. He was worried about her. She made an effort to put on a tranquil and composed face. She didn't want him to worry about her or to think she couldn't handle stress.

"I don't know many people here yet. My best friend from high school and college, Lorena, went to do graduate studies at a program in Rome. She left two months ago. She'll be there for two years. I don't have any siblings, and my cousins are all much younger than I am, since my parents were the oldest of their families, and their siblings all waited to start families."

"Where are your parents?"

"They live in San Antonio. Right now, they're on a month-long cruise to the South Pacific celebrating their thirtieth anniversary. They've never traveled before, and they were looking forward to this trip. I don't want to worry them. I'll send them an email later."

"If you decide that you want to talk, my ears are open." He leaned forward in his chair and gently patted her twice on the knee.

Martha smiled at him, grateful for his concern. She ran her hands nervously through her heavy brown hair and considered his offer. Maybe she could talk to him. After work. Maybe. If she could make herself say anything at all about what was going on in her head.

Ten minutes later, Detective Monroe appeared from around a door frame with a thick file in his baseball mitt-sized hands. "Sorry to keep you waiting. We've had a break in the case, and I wanted to get a handle on the information before we met. Could you come with me?"

"Martha, do you want me to come or wait here?" Bill asked as Martha jumped up to go.

Detective Monroe paused and glanced at Bill with raised eyebrows curiously, waiting for Martha's answer.

"Oh, Detective Monroe, this is Bill Gelise. He's my manager at work. I'm going to be staying with him and his wife for a few days. Do you mind if he comes along? Since he's volunteered to take me in, he should know what I've gotten myself into."

"Pleased to meet you, Sir," said the big detective, smiling politely, but disinterestedly down at Bill and shaking his hand. "You're welcome to come with us." Detective Monroe stood outside the doorway and directed them into a small meeting room. As they walked through the police station, Monroe automatically ducked his head as they passed through door frames. Once they were all seated around a small utilitarian table in the meeting room, Detective Monroe opened his file.

"Facial recognition software found a match to your man. Carrollton is putting a rush on the blood tests from the sample found at your apartment to see if we can confirm it, but your sketch description and the video match this man," he said, offering a picture to Martha. "Do you recognize him?"

Martha only needed an instant to look before she nodded. "That's the gunman, the man who shot Curt Holliczek. Do you know who he is?"

"We do. His name is Marcos Rudolpho Rios Gutierrez. He is a known mercenary from South America, tied to one of the big drug cartels in Peru and suspected in several drug-related murders, as well as in kidnapping for ransom schemes. He's linked to the kidnapping and murder of several European oil-field workers in the Amazon region last year. That region has been unstable, with the indigenous people fighting development of any kind and various oil companies competing to get into it. Officials originally blamed the oil-field kidnappings on the indigenous tribes, but later, evidence pointed to industrial sabotage. Rios may have been working for a competing oil company or even a drug lord with fields in the area. We understand he works for the highest bidder."

"Why would a person like that be car-jacking or mugging someone in Dallas?" asked Bill.

"He wouldn't. We feel we're missing some connection. The attack must have been targeted. Interpol wants Rios in connection to the killing of the oil-field workers. It looks like the FBI will probably want to take the case. They're not happy that Rios managed to get into the country without anyone noticing."

"I saw the victim's wife and his brother, Daniel, leaving when I arrived. I'd met them at the hospital when I went to find out how Mr. Holliczek was recovering. Did you show them this picture?" asked Martha.

"No, we showed them the video from the tunnel. They claim not to recognize Mr. Rios or the other man in the video. This information came in right after they left. Nevertheless, given that the victim was targeted for some reason, we will have to thoroughly investigate the Holliczek family. Our preliminary information shows that Mrs. Holliczek was born in Peru, although she has obtained U.S. citizenship. She and her husband have traveled to Peru twice in the last five years. I recommend that you minimize any contact with the family for the time being."

"Oh, no." Martha's shoulders drooped. Her brain was in turmoil. She not only wanted to see Daniel again, but she hadn't realized until then how much she was looking forward to seeing Alegria. Alegria was sweet and kind and friendly. Martha could see Alegria as a potential friend. Now all that potential was evaporating. Daniel had saved her life, but his family could be involved in murders, kidnappings, and drug cartels. His amber eyes were imprinted on her brain. Pain seared her chest. She felt as if she couldn't inhale.

Bill and Martha drove to the office in silence. Bill tried to ask Martha a question or two, but after getting single-word responses, he gave up. Martha fought to keep from crying.

Martha wanted to crawl into bed and sleep until tomorrow. Back at her desk, she looked over her lists of updates to complete and her priority case objectives. Everything seemed like it would take a year to finish. Work that had been easy to start and finish three days ago now seemed impossible. Time slipped by as she stared at her computer, checked her email, and only managed to pay lost wages for one injured worker. Eight more files needed review, but their deadlines were later. Normally, Martha would have done them all at once. Today, she couldn't focus enough to do any at all.

Bill walked up to her desk. "What time should we expect you? We're having pot roast with potatoes and carrots at six-thirty tonight, if you'd like to join us. Please come. Heidi said to tell you that she's looking forward to meeting you."

Martha squirmed in her chair and fidgeted with the pen in her hand. Her brain was screaming that she'd make terrible company for them, as tired as she was and as shy as she was. "I need to go by and check out of my hotel. Then, I want to ask the police if I can go back to my apartment and collect a few more things. Thank you for the offer of dinner, but I'll be a little too late. I'll grab something to eat by myself. If you'd like, I can bring some dessert, maybe between seven-thirty and eight o'clock?"

"Okay, dessert then. We'll see you tonight." Bill waved and headed back to his office.

Martha closed down her work files and turned off the monitor screen. She picked up her purse and stared at the phone. She wanted to call Daniel. She'd been expecting him to call her since yesterday. The idea that the police didn't want her to talk to him was still painful.

She took the elevator down to the lobby. As she reached the big glass doors to exit the building, her cell phone began to ring in her purse.

Martha cleared the lump forming in her throat and felt her heart begin to race as she answered the phone. The number was unfamiliar. "Hello?"

"Martha? This is Daniel."

"Hi." She paused. Now that he'd called, she didn't know what to say. She couldn't blurt out that the police suspected his family of being involved with drug trafficking and murder.

Daniel's voice filled her head, bridging the gap of silence. "I'm sorry I didn't call sooner. Things got busy. Felix came down with a fever yesterday, so Alegria couldn't stay with Curt at the hospital. Curt came down with a fever, and needed more surgery to see if they'd missed something. I was at the hospital all day yesterday with Curt. He's awake but in pain, which is partly his fault, since he doesn't like pain medicine."

"I'm so sorry to hear that the baby is sick. Is Curt okay? Did the doctors find what was causing the fever?" asked Martha, worried that some complication might kill Curt.

"The doctor said that he cleaned the wound and removed some dead tissue. He said that sort of thing is common with an injury like Curt's. Curt seemed like his usual self after the procedure. Don't worry. He'll be fine," said Daniel. "He's doing much better today. In fact, I'm at the hospital now.

"I saw you and Alegria leaving the police station," said Martha, hoping he'd tell her more about why someone from Peru would attack Curt.

"You were there? I didn't see you. We went in because the police said that they had video of the gunman. We didn't recognize him at all. I'm not sure where the video came from either. The detective wouldn't tell us anything."

"The police got the video because I saw the gunman at lunch today, when I was downtown," said Martha.

"Was he following you again?" asked Daniel sharply, an edge of concern in his voice.

"No, I don't think so. I think we ran into each other by accident. In any case, I saw the video too, and the man in it is definitely the person who shot Curt."

Daniel went silent for a second. Martha could almost hear him assimilating the information. "The police must have identified the man in the video then. Alegria called me to ask me to check on Curt for her since she couldn't get to the hospital. The police showed up at her house and began questioning her about every trip to Peru she and Curt have ever taken," he said.

Martha bit her lip and made a decision. Daniel couldn't be involved in hurting his own brother. She had to tell him what was going on. "Detective Monroe identified the gunman as a Peruvian gun for hire, a mercenary who once worked for a major drug cartel. A guy like that doesn't car-jack or mug someone in Dallas. They think that Curt was targeted for some reason." She inhaled deeply. "I ... I don't think I was supposed to tell you that. In fact, the police advised me to stay away from your family." Martha hesitated to go on, waiting for his response.

"Thank you for telling me. That explains why they're giving Alegria the third degree. I appreciate your trust."

Martha felt herself blush, glad Daniel couldn't see it. "If you can't trust the person who saved your life, who can you trust?" She took a breath and went back to the problem at hand. "Do you think someone in Peru might have a reason to harm Curt?"

"It's unlikely. I don't know who or why ... or wait, maybe I do have an idea. Listen, you've given me an idea that I want to run by Alegria. I should call now while the police are still at the house with her. Can I call you again later?"

"Yes, of cour—"

"Okay, bye." He cut her off and the line went dead.

Martha was left with the word "goodbye" hanging on her lips, wondering what idea he could possibly have had to discuss with Alegria.

Martha shoved her phone back into her purse and headed for the DART depot. Her thoughts bouncing from Daniel to Alegria to Curt and back again, she noticed a dark-haired man, his large stomach stretching the front of his shirt, leaning on the wall bordering the handicapped entrance to the building across the street. She watched him carelessly flick his cigarette into the gutter and mentally condemned him for littering while pitying his addiction. He crossed the street and continued in the direction Martha was walking. Martha thought he looked a little like the man who'd run behind her and missed the bus yesterday, but her mind wandered back to Daniel and Alegria. She focused on hurrying to catch her bus and forgot the man.

Chapter 6

Martha sat on the bus going to the Park and Ride near her hotel. Every seat was full, and a few tall, sturdy souls stood in the aisle holding the overhead bar. Short people often had trouble reaching the top bar, and had to either find seats or spots near the poles. Since she didn't usually take the bus to Addison, none of the faces around her were familiar. Most of the people were engrossed with their phones, tablets, or books; Martha dismissed them as harmless commuters, like her. When she used the Park and Ride near home, she saw the same faces almost every morning and evening on the train. She hadn't spoken to any of them yet, but usually they all nodded politely to each other when waiting for the train.

Martha settled back in her seat and closed her eyes. Her brain was whirling.

Will the police be angry at me for talking to Daniel? How is Curt doing? How sick is Felix? What is Daniel's idea about the attack on Curt?

She exited the bus in turn with all the other riders at the parking lot. The crowd dispersed rapidly in all directions, like puppies escaping a kennel, to various parked cars and waiting vehicles. One dark-haired man flagged down a car to come pick him up.

Martha remembered that she was supposed to pay attention to her surroundings and scanned the parking lot before approaching her car. She checked the back seat before unlocking and opening the door. Sighing, she started the engine and backed out of her parking space. Joining the ant-line of cars leaving the lot, Martha crawled inch by inch, bumper to bumper, to the exit, yielded to oncoming traffic, and swung out onto the street. Her hotel wasn't far, a few minutes down the rush-hour-packed streets.

As she slowed to turn into the hotel parking lot, Martha heard brakes squealing in the lane next to hers as a driver tried to avoid hitting the car that had cut him off. She didn't even turn to see the offending car. Impatient and aggressive drivers were the rule at that point in the day, not the exception.

After parking by the door, Martha went up to her room to collect her belongings. With that task accomplished and the drawers and edges of the bed checked, Martha went down to the hotel's front desk.

"I need to check out. I know it's late in the day, but something came up, and I don't have to stay another night after all." She smiled at the rotund clerk as she put her purse down on the counter.

"Well, you're in luck. Midweek like this, we're mostly empty. I can waive the charge for an additional night. What room?" He typed mechanically and slowly on the keyboard before him, each finger wider than the key it was trying to hit.

"208."

After a minute or two of the laborious typing, he asked, "Martha Rowan?"

She nodded, "Yes."

"I've got a printout for you to sign. The total is here. Sign right here on this line." He set the paper before her and plunked a bratwurst-sized middle finger down on a line near the bottom of the sheet.

She scrawled her signature. He took the sheet and handed her a duplicate. "Thank you for staying with us. Come see us again." He smiled at her with three jolly chins.

"Thanks." Martha threw her purse on her shoulder and went back out to her car. A car was parked in the portico outside the lobby. Martha didn't give it a glance.

After glancing at the instructions for driving to Bill's, Martha considered where to get dinner and set out for the Colombian food restaurant where she'd eaten with Daniel. Thinking about the menu made her mouth water. The *chuzo mixto*, a shish kebab platter, sounded delicious. Besides, the restaurant was closer to I-35 East, which she would need to take to get to Bill's house in Lewisville. Lewisville was yet another of the many suburbs around Dallas and Fort Worth that comprised what locals called "The DFW Metroplex."

Martha pulled out of her parking space and paused at the parking lot exit, yielding to the heavy flow of oncoming traffic on Beltline Road. She watched the cars steadily, waiting for her chance. Barely noticing the car that was pulling up behind her, Martha slid quickly into an opening that materialized and drove toward the restaurant.

Traffic was heavy, a bumper-to-bumper sea of cars idling at each red light that shot forward in choreographed waves the instant a green light appeared. Martha drove forward in unison with her wave, watching the tail lights ahead of her and the lane-change signals around her. Her ears noted honking horns as a car drove aggressively somewhere behind her. As she approached another intersection, the honking of annoyed drivers was continuing and getting louder. The light in front of Martha turned yellow. The car in front of her accelerated to race through the tail end of the yellow light as it turned red. Martha released the gas pedal to begin stopping.

A violent thud shook her small car as someone hit her from behind. Her heart began to pound. She stood on her brake pedal fiercely and gripped the wheel with all her strength as cars began to move through the intersection, crossing in front of her. The car behind her accelerated and hit her car a second time, pushing her forward into the oncoming traffic.

Martha looked left and saw a flash of the face of the middle-aged man driving the large white sedan that was about to hit her. Horror and fear registered in his face. Their eyes met for a millisecond. Martha whipped the steering wheel to the right as hard as she could. She was too late.

The sedan hit her car almost fully broadsided. The force of the impact began to roll her car. Martha barely had time to think, "Oh, no, I'm going to roll," and "Oh, not again," as the car rolled once and then twice before coming to a stop in the grassy median between the lanes of cars.

Martha's ears were ringing with the sounds of crunching metal and screaming. Air bags had exploded around her. Winded and disoriented, Martha felt as though the world were still rotating sideways. A second later, she spat safety glass from her mouth and wondered how it had gotten there.

The car engine was still running, so she turned it off. She began to shake as people appeared outside her car window, which was suddenly open. Glass covered her clothes, the seat around her, and the floor. Every window was broken except for the windshield.

"Are you okay? Where are you hurt?" a young woman was asking.

"I don't know."

"Hold still. I called 911. Help should be here soon," said a black-haired, olive-skinned man holding a cell phone.

Martha moved her legs experimentally. They seemed okay. She turned her head and tested her neck—again okay. She raised her right hand to her forehead and felt a slick, damp area above her left eye. Martha unbuckled her seatbelt with her right hand and began to reach for the door handle with her left hand, when she realized that her left arm was not obeying the command to move. It didn't hurt at all, but she couldn't raise the arm. Gingerly, she checked her fingers. They each moved properly. Then, her elbow. It bent correctly. The problem was with her shoulder.

Martha reached across herself with her right arm to try the door again, but the door wouldn't budge.

The woman outside, a slender, twenty-something blonde in a spaghetti-strapped yellow sundress, spoke again. "The door is crushed. The fire department may need to pry it open."

Martha leaned her head back to wait. A wave of fear exploded across her brain, and tears began to roll down her cheeks. She glanced around. People were milling around everywhere, gawking at the wreck that was her car. At least no one could get at her with this many witnesses standing around her. The cars in all directions had come to a standstill, the rush to get home replaced by the rush of witnessing a terrible wreck. Martha shuddered. Even more people would have been standing around if she'd died.

Sirens sounded, and firemen brought "the jaws" to free Martha from the crushed metal surrounding her. A slow stream of rubbernecking drivers began to trickle past as emergency medical technicians evaluated Martha in her vehicle, placed her on a backboard, and moved her to the waiting ambulance.

Following her first ambulance ride, Martha found herself being examined in a North Carrollton emergency room. A nurse had helped her remove her clothes and put on a hospital gown. Someone had called an orderly to sweep up the glass that had fallen from places hidden within her clothes. Tiny, sparkling, jewel-like cubes of safety glass had insinuated themselves into every conceivable nook and cranny. Bruises now covered her body like an ugly gray-and-purple rash. A nurse cleansed and bandaged the small gash above her left eyebrow. A doctor said she had a mild concussion, and had her arm placed in a temporary sling.

A blue curtain hung across the cubicle-sized hospital treatment area. Martha leaned back on her bed and waited to get her shoulder X-rayed. She was exhausted, slightly dazed, stiff with a headache, sore, and scared. A steady stream of nurses, doctors, and others with papers for her to fill out and sign moved around the blue privacy curtain in front of her bed.

If she'd had an ounce of energy left for worrying about anything else, the sign in bold red letters urging precautions against the spread of MRSA would have bothered her. Given that someone was trying to kill her, worrying about a staph infection was pointless. A pair of Carrollton police officers arrived to ask questions, and Martha directed them to Lieutenant Silk, the Carrollton detective assigned to investigate the attack at her apartment.

Luckily, she'd left Addison and was in Carrollton when the car accident had happened, so Lieutenant Silk would be handling the accident inquiry. Martha had never had so many dealings with police departments before, and throwing in a third one would have been overwhelming. As it was, she had to explain everything at least twice.

An hour after she arrived at the hospital, Lieutenant Silk ambled into her curtained cubicle.

"Hello again, Ms. Rowan," said Silk in his smooth Louisiana drawl. "We've had quite a few witnesses come forward to describe your car accident. Though, of course, it wasn't an accident. The driver of the other car clearly intended to injure or kill you." His eyebrows came together in concern as his eyes took in the sling on her arm and the small cuts on her face.

"Was the driver Rios?" asked Martha.

"No. We showed his picture to several of the witnesses, and none of them identified him. Three of the witnesses had a clear view of the driver and the passenger in the car that forced you out into the intersection. Your friend Monroe over in Dallas sent me the video he had of Mr. Rios, and two of the witnesses said that the driver of the car is the second man in the video. The passenger hasn't been identified yet, but we have the witnesses working with sketch artists now."

Martha supposed she was lucky. Rios himself probably would have shot her.

Lieutenant Silk said, "Every department in the area is looking for the vehicle that hit you. We've got a good description of the vehicle, and several people even wrote down the license plate number. The license plates were stolen, so we don't know who the registered owner of the vehicle is yet. However, I feel confident we'll spot the car quickly."

Martha wasn't reassured. She figured that the driver and passenger would dump the car and hide out. The car would be found somewhere, abandoned, cleaned out, or torched.

Lieutenant Silk said, "Every law enforcement agency in the state and the four surrounding states are hunting for Rios. He can't leave the country. Everyone crossing the border to Mexico will be rigorously checked. He's in a tightening net. It won't be long before he makes a mistake and we catch him."

Martha didn't respond. Rios might get caught, but how many others had he sent after her? Would she be safe anywhere?

Lieutenant Silk seemed to know where her thoughts were going, "I've got an officer in the hall to keep an eye on you while you are here in the hospital. We can assign an officer to watch over you, or put you in protective custody."

"I'm going to stay with my boss and his wife. They've offered to take me in."

A familiar balding head peeked around the blue curtain. "May I come in?" Bill asked hesitantly.

"Bill, please, come on in. Thank you so much for coming. Bill, this is Lieutenant Silk. He was offering to put me in protective custody or assign a guard to me, but if I'm staying at your place, I don't think that's needed. I don't think anyone could follow me there. These people who are after me won't know where I'm staying.

"Hello, Lieutenant. I'm Bill Gelise," said Bill, shaking the police officer's hand. "I'm pretty sure we can keep Martha safe at my house. No one will know where she's staying." He paused a moment, thinking. "But when she's downtown, working, that's different. They know she goes there and probably have a general idea of what areas she frequents. Someone to keep an eye on her there might not be a bad idea."

"If they followed me from downtown, they know I took the bus. They'll watch the bus stops and train stops," said Martha.

"Then I'll drive you to work with me. You should avoid public transportation for a while," said Bill.

"I agree," said Lieutenant Silk. "Don't follow any regular patterns. Don't go anywhere alone. I'll see if Dallas can assign someone to watch your office. I don't know their budget over there. They might only be able to have someone swing by when you're coming and going. Still, that would be better than nothing."

"Sounds good to me," said Bill.

"Well, Ma'am, get some rest. We'll have more paperwork for you to fill out, but it can wait until tomorrow. Come see me and we'll go over everything," said Silk.

"Okay. I'll see you tomorrow," said Martha.

The lieutenant nodded his goodbye, pushed his way around the blue curtain, and was gone.

Bill looked at Martha, "How are you? Anything broken?" His eyes swept over the bandage on her forehead and down to the sling on her left arm.

"I don't know. They haven't X-rayed me yet. I can't raise my left arm. The elbow and hand are fine. I only have pain when I try to move my shoulder."

"How's your head?"

"Sore. I have a mild concussion."

"You made the local news. Prior to the accident, some guys in a car near you were bothered by the aggressive driving of the car that hit you. So one of them took video with his phone. He was trying to catch the driver doing something illegal, and ended up recording the entire incident. It's shaky, but you can see that they were trying to kill you. I don't recommend you watch the video. It's disturbing enough for me to see it. You probably shouldn't relive it."

"Maybe I should go to a hotel. I don't want to put you and your wife in any danger."

"Don't even think of it. I've got a great alarm system on the house and a hunting rifle in my closet. This is Texas. If an intruder comes into my house, I can shoot him. Don't be afraid I'd miss, either. I grew up on a farm in East Texas shooting cans for fun and rabid animals for protection." He settled into the chair next to the bed and reached out to pat her undamaged arm.

Two HOURS, ONE X-ray, three nurses, and forty signatures later, Martha and Bill left the hospital. Bill drove and Martha dozed in his car all the way to his house. She awoke disoriented as the car came to a stop in the driveway of a red-brick, two-story home with stone accents in a well-manicured neighborhood. Miniature rose bushes lined the drive, and a three-foot-square rosemary bush filled the small space between the drive and the small walk up to the front door. Hanging baskets of moss roses drooped down from hooks on the porch.

"Here we are. Do you need any help, or can you get out by yourself?"

"It might take me longer than usual, but I can manage. Thanks," Martha assured him.

The front door flew open and a small woman in a broom skirt and embroidered peasant top appeared almost instantly beside the car. She had the car door open and was helping Martha out before Martha realized what was going on.

The woman spoke quickly and quietly. "Welcome to our house. Let me help you. That accident looked terrible, but don't worry anymore, you'll be safe here with us." Her short, graying hair curled around her ears. The small lines at the corners of her eyes and a slight heaviness around her jawline marked her age as closer to fifty than forty, but her energy made her seem much younger.

"Thank you."

The woman reminded Martha of a small, delicate bird. She flitted around Martha, closed the car door, and led her into the house. Martha was seated in a chair with extra pillows and a drink on a small table at her elbow, and then offered food in a heartbeat.

Bill performed the introductions. "In case you haven't realized it yet, this is my wife, Heidi. She's missed mothering our daughter since she left for college." He paused and winked at his wife.

"It's a pleasure to meet you, Ma'am. Thank you, but I hate to be such trouble for you," said Martha.

"Call me Heidi. Now, did you decide if you're hungry?" Heidi clasped her hands in front of her, awaiting Martha's response with the look of an eager volunteer, happy to be allowed to help.

"I was on my way to dinner when the accident happened. I should probably eat something, but I don't feel very hungry."

"How about some pot roast cut up in a bowl with beef broth, rice, and vegetables? It'll make a tasty soup. I could have it for you in a minute or two."

"That sounds wonderful." Martha smiled as Heidi flitted out of the room again. Watching Heidi was like watching a hummingbird; even when she stood still, she exuded vibrant energy.

Heidi returned with the beef soup in the blink of an eye, placing it on the small table next to Martha's uninjured right arm with her drink. Martha sat sipping slowly and listened while Bill explained her injuries to Heidi.

"Well, the arm isn't broken, but she separated her shoulder. The doctor said she'd have to follow up with her own doctor and probably go to physical therapy. She has bumps and bruises all over, and the small cut you see on her forehead. They think she has a mild concussion, so no rough sports until she heals. Right, Martha?" He smiled at her, trying to get her to respond to his joke.

"Right, no football or soccer." She gave him a tired smile, and ate a bite of pot roast from her soup.

"How is your head, Martha?" asked Heidi.

"Achy, but not too bad. They gave me pain medicine at the hospital."

"Take your time and eat. I've got Dora's room all ready for you when you're ready for bed," Heidi said.

Heidi changed the subject to her upcoming book club meeting, and then to Dora, chatting quietly with Bill while Martha finished eating.

Martha looked around and took in the details of her boss's house while she ate. She was ensconced in a cozy, pale-yellow, overstuffed chair in a spacious living room. A cream-colored sofa with two reclining seats built into it and two cherry-wood-stained rocking chairs completed the seating area. The floor was laminate wood in a rich cherry color. An intricately patterned Persian rug in golden yellows and reds covered the floor in the seating area. Golden-colored curtains covered a large picture window that in the daytime gave a view of the front yard and neighborhood. A valance patterned in red and gold hid the curtain rod. A framed copy of a Monet *Haystack* painting hung next to a richly colored and textured copy of a Mary Cassatt painting of a mother and child on the wall opposite the window.

A glass-faced curio that was five feet across stood against the far wall. The top shelf held photos of a girl and reflected her growth from infancy to adulthood. Happy baby pictures snuggled next to high school graduation and prom pictures, with gap-toothed photos and awkward tween photos peeking around them.

The second and third shelves held an assortment of pottery. Martha recognized small pieces of southwestern Native American pottery, some that looked Asian and others that might be African. She didn't know enough about pottery to even begin to guess what countries or groups or tribes made each style.

"Do you like my collection?" asked Heidi, noticing how Martha was studying it. "I love pottery. I make some of my own as a hobby, but I like to collect examples of different types as well."

"It's a wonderful collection." Martha set her soup bowl down on the table at her elbow and rose painfully to look at the pottery.

"Fortunately, Bill likes to travel. In the twenty-five years we've been married, we've been all around the world for vacations. Wherever we go, I pick up an example of the local pottery. I've amassed quite a lot over the years. What you see are what I consider my best pieces. More pieces are scattered around the house, with the bulk of them in my pottery work-shop, which is also known as the garage."

The phone rang in the Gelise kitchen. At first Martha didn't realize she was hearing a ring tone. She heard the theme to the musical *Oklahoma!* playing suddenly and looked around to find the source.

Chapter 7

By the time Martha located the phone, Heidi already had it in her hand and was saying, "Hello?"

"I don't know who could be calling this late," Bill said to Martha. "It's almost midnight. You must be exhausted. We've kept you up too late." He started to say something more, but Heidi interrupted.

"Martha, it's for you. Detective Monroe is calling."

Martha walked haltingly, her body aching, to the phone. "Hello?"

"Hello, Ms. Rowan, this is Detective Monroe."

"Hi. Is there something you need? Did something new turn up? Did you find the car that hit me?"

"We're still working a lead on that. I'm calling about the attack on Mr. Holliczek. Border Patrol in El Paso reports that they've taken Marcos Rios into custody. They caught him at a border crossing with fake identification about an hour ago. That confirms the witnesses' reports that he wasn't in the car that hit you. It's a nine-hour drive from here to El Paso. He'd have to have left town right after you saw him at lunchtime."

"Oh, that's great that he's been caught!" Martha's mouth stopped working. Her brain was three steps ahead of her mouth, which wouldn't cooperate. "I ... Did ... Do ... What do ..."

"We're hoping we'll get some answers out of him regarding the situation here, but the international and federal charges he's facing will take precedence over the attempted murder and other charges he's facing here in Dallas. I wanted you to know that he's not out there, lurking around. You should remain with Mr. Gelise tonight, though. If my lead on Mr. Rios' associate pans out, we should have him in custody shortly, but until then, you shouldn't return to your apartment."

"Oh, yes, I understand." Martha paused. She had a million questions about Rios and what kind of leads the police were pursuing, but all she could say was, "Thank you. You'll let me know when you think it's safe for me to go back to my apartment, won't you?"

"Yes, I'll call when I have more information."

"Oh, thank you, Detective. Goodnight."

Martha turned to face Bill and Heidi, who were waiting by the sofa in the living room. "They caught Marcos Rios, the gunman who shot Curt Holliczek. The Border Patrol arrested him when he tried to cross the border in El Paso."

Heidi clapped her hands together and gave a small cheer while Bill responded, "That's great news!"

"Detective Monroe said not to go home yet, though. He says they are still working on getting his associates. Rios couldn't have been in the car that hit me. It's a nine-hour drive to El Paso from here. He must have sent someone else after me."

"You stay here with us for as long as you need, dear." Heidi came and put an arm around Martha, avoiding her injured shoulder. "We can talk more tomorrow. You'll stay here with me and rest. It'll be Friday, and you'll have a long weekend to recover from that accident. For now, let's get you to bed. Come with me. I'll help you get changed."

Heidi led Martha to Dora's forsaken bedroom. The room obviously belonged to a teenaged girl. Movie posters covered one wall. Awards and trophies for volleyball and piano filled a shelf along the ceiling. A cork board was filled with photos of teenage girls and boys, some making silly faces for the camera.

Here and there, empty spaces on the wall and cleared shelves on the bookcase gave evidence of items having been removed haphazardly by their young owner. Where visible, the walls were painted lavender. Matching lavender-and-cornflower curtains were draped around the window above a small writing desk.

"The bedspread and sheets are all new," said Heidi, patting the purple, floral-patterned bedspread covering the twin bed. "Dora took her favorites with her. I need to get another clock in here, too." She pointed to the empty night stand next to the bed. "Dora took her alarm clock. I hope it's getting her to those eight a.m. classes on time. She was never a morning person. Getting up early during a summer session is probably extra difficult for her."

Martha wanted to refuse Heidi's help in changing her clothes, but she couldn't raise her left arm at all. Exhaustion and painkillers had removed her inhibitions as much as a few glasses of alcohol would have. She sat on the twin bed and allowed Heidi to help her raise her shirt over her head.

"Oh, my!" said Heidi, the crow's feet around her happy eyes deepening and creases layering her forehead as she saw the bruises covering Martha's torso. The bruise from the seat belt was an ugly purple across Martha's left shoulder and chest. Dozens of smaller bruises spotted her back and sides.

"It's okay, Heidi. I don't feel the bruises. I got a heavy dose of ibuprofen at the hospital, so nothing hurts much right now. I'm only feeling stiff."

"Martha, let me put some arnica ointment on the bruises. You'll heal faster. My doctor says it will help clear up the bruising itself, too, so you won't have all the dark purple everywhere. It's a homeopathic remedy, plant based. I'm a bit of a nature child. My doctor knows how to take the best of modern and ancient medicine and recommend what works. I trust her judgment on these things. She recommended arnica to me after I had a bad fall from a ladder two years ago. I was a mass of bruises. Let me get some for you. I'll be right back." She zipped out of the room.

Heidi smeared the ointment over the worst of the bruises, and Martha crawled into bed.

The next thing she knew, it was Friday morning.

Martha sat up stiffly. Her joints ached, especially her shoulder. The sun was fully up and shining in a bright halo around the edges of the blinds. A glance at her phone confirmed it was already nine. She should have been to work an hour ago, except she didn't have a car, and the doctor had said to rest today.

Martha fell back on the pillow and took stock. Most of her aches were mild. She needed to make a list of things to get done, the first items being to deal with her car insurance company and rent a car. Though it wasn't official yet, according to the insurance company, she knew by the condition she'd left it in that her car was totaled, which meant she'd eventually have to get a new one. She exhaled heavily, knowing she would miss her car.

Her phone on the night stand beside the bed began to ring. Martha reached for it, wincing as she rolled on her injured left shoulder, and answered.

"Hello?"

"Martha, hi, it's Alegria. Detective Monroe called to tell us that they caught that man, Rios, who shot Curt," she said. The happiness in her voice was unmistakable.

"Hi, Alegria. Yes, I know. He called me, too. Did he tell you about my car accident?" asked Martha.

"No! What happened?" Alegria said.

"I was driving to a friend's place last night when a car rear-ended my car and pushed me into oncoming traffic. My car rolled. My friend tells me the whole thing made the news last night." Martha sat on the edge of the bed. She found a pair of slippers on the floor under her feet and slid into them.

"Oh, no, no, no! That was you? I saw that on the news. That has to be the worst thing I've ever seen in my life that wasn't really a movie. Do they know who did it? Is it connected to my husband's shooting?" Alegria sounded near tears.

"It must be. It may have been another attempt to remove me as a witness. Rios must have sent the people in the car that hit me. He couldn't have done it himself because he was already on his way to El Paso by the time the accident happened. Detective Monroe said they were working on a lead to Rios' associates." Martha realized she didn't know whether that meant the man she'd seen in the tunnel or the people in the car that had hit her, or both. She wished she'd asked more questions.

Alegria didn't answer.

"Alegria, are you still there?" asked Martha.

"Yes, I am disappointed. I thought, when they caught this man Rios, it was over. I didn't realize that others were working with him. You are still in danger, and, perhaps, we are also, if he left others to finish whatever he started." Alegria's voice cracked.

"Please don't cry. The police will round up everyone involved soon." Martha shifted uncomfortably. Now that she was sitting up, pain was beginning to flare through her body from a thousand points, and her shoulder throbbed with a dull but growing ache. Concentrating on Alegria's words suddenly became difficult.

"That accident was so terrible. You are in danger because you helped my husband. We must help you."

"Wait, no, no, no. You have enough to do. Tomorrow is Saturday, and I'm not going to work today. I don't need any help. My manager from work has already volunteered to help me get around until I get a new car. You don't owe me anything. Daniel says we're even since I saved Curt, and he saved me."

"Daniel said ... Daniel doesn't get to decide."

"Alegria, this isn't your fault. You don't have to do anything," Martha said, interrupting.

Alegria didn't seem to hear Martha. "You must come to dinner at my house. Can you come tomorrow night? I will send Daniel to pick you up. Please, come."

"Okay, what time?" Martha asked. The throbbing in her shoulder was intensifying, and she wanted the conversation to end so she could go find some pain medicine.

"Is six-thirty too early?" asked Alegria.

"No, that's fine." Martha was about to end the conversation, but bit back her goodbye. She suddenly remembered that Daniel had thought of something that might explain the attack on Curt.

"Um, Alegria? Daniel said he had thought of something that might help the police, something that might explain why Curt was attacked. I don't mean to be nosy, but I've been wondering what it was." She cradled her injured arm against her body and rubbed it with her right hand, balancing the phone between her neck and shoulder.

"Oh, he remembered about my Tío in Peru. He defies the drug cartel. The police said they would look into it. Perhaps, now that they have caught this man Rios, he will say who hired him. We are afraid he was trying to kidnap little Felix to force my Tío to do something or to make him pay ransom."

"Oh, I see." A wave of relief went through Martha. They weren't part of a drug cartel. They were fighting it.

Martha said goodbye and lay back on the bed with her shoulder aching and a crick in her neck from holding the phone. She needed to call her insurance company. She needed to follow up with a doctor about her shoulder, but she hadn't seen a doctor since moving to town. She'd have to select one. Rolling over onto her good shoulder, Martha pushed herself up with her good arm. First, the pain medicine. Quickly.

In the kitchen, Martha found Heidi wearing leggings and a thigh-length, oversized T-shirt, standing by the sink, slipping cups into the dishwasher. The kitchen was painted moss green with a matching green tile backsplash running under mounted maple cabinets. Interspersed with the green were decorative tiles that depicted various herbs and spices. The countertops were white and gray Corian. Morning sunlight streamed in through a window behind the sink, providing light for a row of purple, flowering African violets.

"You're up! I was hoping you'd sleep longer. Can I get you some breakfast? Eggs? Pancakes? Cereal? Toast? I also have coffee, juice, milk, or a variety of tea bags for hot tea, if you prefer?" Heidi said brightly.

Martha smiled at Heidi and shook her head. "You're spoiling me with options. Cereal and toast are fine. I do like hot tea. What kinds do you have?"

"Take your pick." Heidi held open a wooden box of individually wrapped and labeled tea bags.

By the time Martha had selected an Irish Breakfast tea, Heidi had laid the round pine table with a bowl, spoons, a mug of steaming water, sugar, milk, and four different varieties of cereal.

"The toast will be ready in a moment. What would you like on it? Butter, grape jelly, strawberry jelly, apricot jam, or cream-cheese spread?"

"Plain butter is fine."

In another moment, Martha was eating, and Heidi sat across from her with a mug of coffee.

"How can I help you out today?" asked Heidi. "My time belongs to you."

"Thanks. I'm supposed to follow up with a doctor about my shoulder, but I don't have a doctor here in town yet. I need to call my insurance company about my car. I'm hoping I can get a rental car until I can buy a new one." Martha took a bite of toast.

"Don't worry about a thing. I'll get you an appointment with my doctor and drive you there. You don't need to rent a car unless you want one. I'm happy to drive you around," Heidi said.

"I don't know when I'll hear from my insurance company about my car or whether it'll even be fixed. I'd better rent a car. I can't have you driving me around for a week or more." Martha looked at Heidi, who was slowly sipping her coffee. She had never seen her sit still. Somehow, she even sat energetically, tapping one foot under the table.

"Do you need help getting dressed? How is your arm today?"

"I can get dressed by myself, if I move slowly and carefully."

"Well, while you get dressed, I'll call and get you an appointment with the doctor. Do you have your insurance card? Give it to me, and I'll take care of everything."

Martha smiled at Heidi gratefully. "I'll get you the card. You are an angel and a wonderful person. I don't know what I would have done without you and Bill."

"We're glad to help." Heidi gave her a beaming smile and began to clear away the empty dishes from the table in front of Martha.

Two HOURS LATER, after completing Lieutenant Silk's pile of paperwork, Martha sat waiting in the office of Dr. Georganna Pierce, family practitioner, with Heidi at her side. Martha was thumbing through an old copy of *Time* when her phone began to ring in her purse. It took her three rings to find it under her wallet, and she was afraid the call had gone to voice mail.

"Hello?" she said quickly.

"Martha? Hi, it's Daniel. Alegria says I have to pick you up for dinner tomorrow. Are you up for it? She told me about your accident. How are you doing?"

Martha could hear the concern in his voice. "I'm fine. I'm at the doctor's office now for a follow-up on my arm. You don't need to pick me up for dinner tomorrow. I'm going to rent a car."

"I'm glad you're okay. I saw the video online, and it looked really bad. If you change your mind or don't feel like driving yourself, call me. I'd be happy to pick you up. Are you still staying at that hotel?" he asked.

A nurse appeared from behind a door in the waiting room and called Martha's name.

"No, I'm staying with Bill and ... Oh, sorry. I'm being called. I have to go to my appointment now. Bye." Martha clicked off the phone and followed the nurse to an examination room, hoping she hadn't offended him by ending the call so abruptly.

Later that night, Martha relaxed on Dora's bed in Bill and Heidi's house. The doctor had been friendly and oozed competence from every pore. Martha had liked her instantly. The rest of the day had been spent taking a long nap after lunch, making phone calls to the insurance company, and arranging to pick up a rental car the next morning. She was glad to discover that her insurance would cover the cost. The agent had even gotten back to her before dinner to inform her that they had categorized her car as a total loss, and would mail a check to her the next day. A quiet dinner with Bill and Heidi, followed by conversation and television, completed the day.

Martha remembered that she had forgotten to call Daniel back. She considered calling him, but her shoulder had begun to ache again, and besides, she would see him the next day. She decided to take some ibuprofen and crawl into the bed.

SATURDAY MORNING CAME, ending a series of nightmares that had lasted through the night. Her brain and memory had intertwined the shootings and the car accident until she felt like she was tumbling in space, being chased, with blood spurting all around. She awoke with a start over the image of blood seeping between her fingers—this time from her own body, not Curt Holliczek's. A warm shower helped block out most of the memories and restored her appetite, but did nothing for the dark circles under her tired eyes. After a leisurely breakfast of bacon, eggs, biscuits, honey, and hot tea, Bill drove Martha to pick up her rental car, a red Chevy Impala.

Bill stood with his arms crossed and frowned at the car as Martha opened the door. He looked strange to Martha's eyes—long and lanky in an old pair of jeans and a plaid, short-sleeved, button-down shirt, instead of solid and formal in his workday slacks and tie. A Texas Rangers baseball cap protected his balding pate from the morning sun. He asked, "Are you sure you want a car? It doesn't seem safe. Maybe you should get something larger, like an SUV."

"They caught Rios. The police will catch his friends. They are probably hiding out instead of looking for me again. Would they be likely to try to cause another accident? I can't imagine being in two car accidents in one week. It doesn't seem possible. This car will work until I can buy a new one. Please, don't worry about me," Martha said. "Thanks for driving me. You go do your errands. You have things to do today, and I've taken up enough of your time. I'm going to pick up a new outfit or two, and then I'll be back to your house before I go to dinner with the Holliczeks." Martha turned to get into the car.

"I thought the police said to avoid contact with them?" Bill said.

"It's okay. They aren't involved in drugs. Alegria said her uncle has been defying the cartel for years. She thinks this all might have been an attempt to kidnap her baby to put pressure on him or to force him to pay a ransom."

"Hmmmm … Well. You be safe driving around today. Keep your eyes open and avoid unpopulated areas." Bill's lips were pressed into a flat line. Martha could see he wasn't happy. He wanted to say more and was biting his lips to keep the words from escaping. If he'd been her father, Martha knew he'd have said much more about following the police's instructions. He was minding his own business, but he was worried.

"I promise I'll be careful. See you later," Martha said. She wanted to reassure him. He hadn't met the Holliczek family. If she were to introduce them, maybe he'd be less worried. She got into the car and waved to him as he climbed back into his truck.

Martha shopped until she found a simple, pale-blue summer dress that flattered her curvy figure. Even more importantly, she could step into the dress, so she didn't have to raise her injured shoulder to put it on. Brands and trends in clothing didn't interest her. She only wanted something that fit comfortably and flattered her curves. Genetics had given her generous curves. She'd never be long and lean like a model, but she wasn't chubby either. Playing sports like volleyball for most of her life had made her athletic with well-toned arm and leg muscles and an attractive, healthy glow to her skin, all of which was accentuated by the little blue sundress and a pair of low-heeled, slip-on sandals. She reasoned that she needed the dress, since the rest of her clothes were stuck in her apartment, but in the back of her mind she knew she wanted something pretty to wear to dinner.

Something Daniel might like. The jeans and T-shirt she had on weren't good enough.

Shopping completed, she returned to Bill and Heidi's house as promised. At Heidi's insistence, Martha took a short afternoon nap. She wasn't feeling as sore as she had been Friday, and didn't think she would sleep. When she awoke an hour later, feeling refreshed, she was glad she had listened to Heidi.

After phoning Alegria and getting her address, Martha slipped carefully into the blue dress, trying to avoid raising her injured arm. The sleeveless dress revealed many of the bruises and scratches on her arms, but they seemed to be healing quickly. Heidi's arnica cream had worked wonders. Martha input the address into the rental car's system. She decided her next car would have to come with a navigation feature. It worked like a charm and got her to Alegria's house in no time at all.

The navigation system told Martha she had reached her destination, but Martha drove past the house. An unknown dark-haired man in gray slacks and a guayabera shirt and a slim, brown-skinned woman in a cream-colored blouse and navy pants stood on the lawn in front of the Holliczek's house arguing loudly. A red sedan was parked on the street in front of the house.

Chapter 8

The neighborhood consisted of twenty- to thirty-year-old, red brick homes, with large trees towering over many houses. Well-tended beds of flowers and flat-topped rows of bushes in every yard gave the neighborhood a feeling of conventional conformity and safety. Lawns of St. Augustine grass spread from the landscaped areas down to the sidewalk-lined street. Martha drove around the block twice without stopping. The man and the woman continued to argue. She glanced at the dashboard clock. She was fifteen minutes early. She was too early as usual, but at least she could wait until the man and woman quit arguing or left.

She considered driving to a nearby store or gas station, but rejected the idea. No point in leaving the area once she was already there. After her third trip around the block, Martha was glad to see the arguing couple had left. The red car had also disappeared. She parked on the street in front of the Holliczeks' house. If she were to drive around the block again, some neighbor would probably think she was casing the area to rob it. She didn't want to look any more conspicuous than she already was.

Sitting in the car applying lipstick and tugging a comb quickly through her long, straight, brown hair, Martha's thoughts began flowing again. She wished she'd told Alegria that she couldn't come. However, she'd said yes. Alegria expected her. It'd be rude not to show up. It wasn't as if it was a large party where no one would notice if she didn't show up. If the arguing couple were inside the house, the evening would be a shambles. Martha couldn't handle any more tension. Going into a house with friendly strangers was hard enough. Hostile strangers she couldn't face.

In college, when she'd been invited to parties for the volunteer and church organizations she'd joined, she'd always had trouble making herself get out of the car and go into the party. Sometimes she didn't make it. She would sit in the car trying to convince herself to go inside, until the disparaging voices in her head won and she went home. The outcome wasn't much different if she did go inside. Most of the time, if she did manage to go in, she ended up sitting on a couch talking to no one or standing by a wall. Somehow, she couldn't make small talk, and walking up to a group of people who were already talking was impossible. Usually, she'd leave within the hour, having spoken no more than a few words to anyone. This behavior had frustrated her friend Lorena, who tried to help, coaxing her out of the car and into a building more than once. Lorena had understood that Martha couldn't help it, that parties somehow panicked her and made her shut down.

Another vehicle came around the corner onto the street. Martha watched as a gray Ford F-150 pulled into the driveway, and she instantly recognized Daniel in the driver's seat. She watched him climb out of his truck. His short dark hair was combed back from his forehead, his face stubbly with a day's growth of beard. Martha wondered if he didn't bother shaving on the weekends. He wore dark blue jeans with a wide leather belt, low on his narrow hips, and a tan polo shirt with a collar. He spotted her, but started to turn to walk to the house.

Martha was disappointed that he hadn't stopped to wait for her. As she watched, he turned around and walked back to her car.

"You are coming in, aren't you?" he asked.

Martha opened the door of her rental car and climbed out. "Yes, I'm coming. I didn't want to be too early." She locked the car with a click of the remote attached to the key.

"How is your shoulder?" Daniel asked.

Martha looked at him. His eyes weren't as bright, and he looked worried. She thought he needed reassuring about her injury. "It's improving. I can lift it, but not over my head. Getting dressed is complicated. No T-shirts or pullovers unless I want to be in pain." Martha demonstrated, raising her arm almost to the level of her shoulder before wincing as she hit her limit.

He seemed withdrawn. He didn't say anything else as they walked up the sidewalk to the house, so Martha tried again.

"The doctor I saw yesterday gave me a big therapy rubber band and a bunch of exercises to do with it. She said if I don't do my exercises, I might develop shoulder adhesions, and an orthopedist would have to do something unpleasant called a 'manipulation' under anesthesia, so that I could move my shoulder again. I start therapy Monday."

"Oh," Daniel reached for the door and opened it. "Come on in."

Daniel still wasn't looking at her. Martha was confused. He'd been so friendly before that the change was startling.

Martha paused on the doorstep, wishing she could go back to her car.

Almost as if he sensed her doubt, Daniel turned and gave her a perplexed smile. "I'm glad you came." As he stepped into the house, Daniel called out, "Alegria, I'm here, and I found Martha out front."

Alegria appeared from the doorway wearing a chocolate-colored skirt made up of several layers of very thin, gauzy material that swung about her knees and a fitted, floral-print blouse. She opened her arms as she walked to Martha, saying,

"Martha, welcome! Come in." She hugged Martha and air-kissed her near the cheek in a traditional Latin American greeting. "Put your purse on this table, and come take a seat. You look lovely! Daniel, doesn't she look nice?"

Daniel glanced at Martha with a restrained smile hovering on his lips. "Yes, she does," he answered politely.

"Did you have any trouble finding the house?" said Alegria, leading Martha to a seating area in front of a fireplace in the living room at the front of the house.

Martha's eyes followed Daniel as he vanished from the room. His behavior was so contradictory, she felt a half step out of time, like the rhythm to the music of her life had skipped in an odd and disconcerting way. She focused on Alegria's question. "No, the car I rented has a navigation system, and it got me here even faster than I thought was possible."

"Daniel would have been happy to pick you up. Where did he go?" she asked, looking around. "He's probably checking on my little Felix."

"Is Felix feeling better?" Martha asked.

"Yes, he has a very runny nose and a small ear infection. The doctor recommended some medicine for him and pre-scribed ear drops, but not antibiotics. He said the infection would clear up on its own. Felix is fine. How are *you* feeling?"

"I'm not as stiff and sore as I was yesterday. I've been to the doctor, and I'll have to do therapy to help my shoulder, but overall I'm great." Martha glanced around the room. Alegria had decorated the walls with woven hangings and paintings depicting mountains and clouds and llamas. Peruvian pottery and knick-knacks were displayed on shelves on the walls. A brown and cream-colored rug made of some kind of long animal fur was spread in front of the brick fireplace hearth on top of the thick, tan, wall-to-wall carpeting. A mocha-colored leather sofa and a darker brown, overstuffed chair created a seating area in front of the fireplace. Martha's nose picked up the faint scent of baby powder and, from somewhere, the scent of cooking food, heavy with garlic and herbs.

Alegria followed Martha's gaze to the rug. "Do you like that rug? Go touch it. It is extremely soft," she said.

Martha hesitated, but got up when Alegria nodded at her to go ahead. She felt the pale-yellow and brown rug with her hand. "That's the softest fur! What is it?" she asked.

"It's alpaca, a kind of llama. Many of them live in the Andes in Peru. People use the fur to make rugs and to weave into sweaters."

Martha returned to the leather sofa as Daniel returned carrying little Felix in the crook of his arm. The baby, olive-skinned, with a mass of thin, tangled, light-brown hair, was wearing a red, one-piece outfit. He'd twisted his little body to look forward as Daniel carried him into the room.

Alegria gave Daniel an exaggerated stage frown. "You didn't wake him up, did you?" She sounded as if she was accusing him of making an enormous error of judgment.

Daniel shot her a look, his amber eyes wide in denial. "You think I don't know enough to let sleeping babies lie? I didn't wake him. He was babbling happily in his crib."

"Did you check and see if he needs changing?" she asked with a teasing note in her voice.

"That I leave to his mother or father. I'm only the uncle," he responded as he put the baby into Alegria's arms.

She checked the baby, declared him ready to play, and handed him back to his uncle who took him across the room to a quilted blanket with toys scattered around it on the floor.

"Now, Daniel said you were staying at a hotel. Have you no family here?" Alegria asked, turning back to Martha.

"I moved here for work three months ago. My parents live in San Antonio, where I grew up," Martha said. "Anyway, I'm not at the hotel anymore. My manager from work offered to let me stay at his place."

A bell began ringing in the distance. "The rice is finished cooking! I must go turn it off and check the rest of the food. I'll be right back," said Alegria.

"It smells delicious," said Daniel. "What are we having?"

Alegria paused on her way out of the room. "Roast chicken with garlic and herbs, *humitas verdes*, salad, rice, and black beans for dinner. Flan for dessert." She ticked the list off on her fingers and then vanished into the adjoining kitchen.

"What are *humitas verdes*?" Martha asked Daniel. "I know *verde* means green, but I don't know the word *humitas*."

"It's a Peruvian corn meal tamale: a corn dough cooked inside a corn husk. I like them," he said.

"How old is Felix?" Martha asked, watching the baby laugh as Daniel tickled his toes.

"He turned one two weeks ago. Do you want to hold him?" Daniel asked, still too politely, but kindly, from his position across the room near the baby.

"I don't have any experience with babies. I'm not even sure *how* to hold him."

"That's not a problem. Neither did I, until this little guy was born. I refused to hold him for about a week because I was afraid I would break him. Curt made me hold him after that. Relax and be confident. He can sense if you're tense or nervous and will cry," Daniel said. He sat the child on Martha's lap and retreated across the room.

Felix looked at Martha with enormous brown eyes rimmed with dark lashes, pulled himself into a standing position on her lap, and grabbed her nose. Martha laughed and moved his hand.

"Here, give him these to play with," said Daniel, walking back over with a set of keys.

"Those are real keys. I thought babies played with plastic ones?" said Martha.

"He wants real stuff now, but you have to be careful what you hand him because—"

At that moment, Felix threw the keys to the ground, which made a satisfying clattering noise. Then, he squealed with delight.

"... his favorite game is pick up," Daniel continued. "He throws stuff, you pick it up and give it back to him, and he throws it again."

Martha handed the keys back to Felix, and he promptly threw them to the floor again.

"I see," said Martha.

"Yes, he throws cups, books, toys, cell phones, keys, spoons, whatever he can get his hands on," said Daniel. "If you had glasses, he'd pull them off your face, taste them, and then throw them. That's how he treats his grandparents. When he isn't hungry, you have to keep your distance in the kitchen, because the food will be flying."

Martha looked back at Daniel and caught him smiling warmly at the thought. His eyes were alight and playful. Then, abruptly, the light went out, and the polite mask returned the second their eyes met. Martha was surprised, but didn't have time to consider the matter because Felix had chosen that second to grab at her eyes and nose. By the time she freed herself, she found Daniel had distanced himself again, standing a good twenty feet away.

Martha giggled as Felix tried to grab her mouth.

"How is Curt today?" she asked once she got her lips free.

Alegria entered the room and started to answer the question at the same time as Daniel.

"You go ahead," Daniel said.

Alegria said, "He is much better today. He is refusing the stronger pain medicine because it makes him sleepy, so they have switched him to ibuprofen. His wound must have follow-up care, but the doctor thinks he can come home in a few days if he doesn't get any more infections. I was with him this morning, and Daniel spent the afternoon with him." She turned to Daniel and asked, "Did Curt behave himself while you were there?"

"Other than insisting that he wanted to get up and walk for a few minutes, he did exactly what the nurse said," Daniel said with a combative sparkle in his eye.

"You let him get up?!" Alegria cried out, a look of horror on her face. "He just had surgery!"

"I made sure he didn't fall after I realized nothing I said was going to keep him in the bed. You know how stubborn he is."

Alegria shook her head. "He is stubborn like a mule! I could have made him stay in bed."

"I'm sure *you* could have. Wives have ways of making their husbands stay in bed, but I'm only the younger brother," Daniel said, grinning at Alegria.

Martha laughed. She was enjoying their bantering.

"You are not funny, Daniel," Alegria said with mock seriousness as she stood up. A telephone was ringing in the kitchen.

Baby Felix babbled, and began to reach down toward the floor.

"He wants down so he can crawl around. Go ahead and put him down. He's almost got walking down. He took his first steps last week," said Daniel.

Martha put Felix on the floor between her feet. He promptly grabbed her knees and pulled himself to his feet.

Just then, Alegria's raised voice was heard coming from the kitchen. "Veronica! *Ven aqui!*" Then her voice lowered and the words became unintelligible, but the sadness in her tone came through clearly.

Martha looked at Daniel, questions on her lips. He was walking toward the kitchen when Alegria and another woman entered the room. Alegria was speaking rapidly in Spanish; tears were flowing down her face. From her tone, Martha thought the other woman was asking questions, or, more probably, demanding answers.

"What's wrong? What's going on?" asked Daniel. "Is it Curt?"

"*No, no, es mi Tío Felipe. Está muerto,*" Alegria said.

"What? Wait. Your uncle died? What happened?" asked Daniel.

"You remember. We talked about how Tío Felipe has trouble with the drug traffickers. I tried to call him after Curt got hurt to see if he had been having more trouble with them," said Alegria. "No one would answer the telephone. He is in a remote area, so we thought maybe the line was down, so I sent an email since he has computer access by satellite. Still I got no answer. Now, my mother has called to say that he was taken to the hospital the day Curt was injured. He had a massive heart attack. It took three hours to get to the nearest hospital. The damage to his heart from the attack was severe. He was unconscious and never woke up. He died today."

"Oh, Alegria, I'm so sorry," Daniel said, walking over to her and to give her a hug.

As Daniel let go of her, Alegria continued, "His maid says a masked man brought a letter to the house. Tío Felipe read the letter and had the attack. The letter was a ransom note about Felix. So, you see, we were right! Someone was trying to kidnap Felix!"

Chapter 9

The other woman, who had been standing behind Alegria, moved forward and put an arm around her. She had the same dark eyes and brown skin as Alegria, but she was taller. Where Alegria was casual and matronly, she was formal and professional. Her cream silk blouse and navy linen slacks were perfectly tailored to her slender figure, and her hair was carefully styled. She looked as though she had never had a hair out of place. Her expression was serious, but she was not crying. Martha recognized her as the woman who had been arguing on the front lawn earlier.

"Martha, this is my sister, Veronica," said Alegria.

"I'm pleased to meet you," Martha said, and then, regretting it, added, "I mean, I'm so sorry for your loss." Her face flushed. She looked at Daniel for a hint of what to do, but he was looking at Alegria.

Martha asked, "Should I go? I know you've had a shock. You probably don't want to entertain a guest right now. Will you be going to the funeral?"

"Martha, no, please stay. I can't do anything from here. The funeral will be tomorrow, and I could not possibly get there in time. Burial is faster in Peru than here. My mother will stay with the body until they bury him after a funeral at the church," said Alegria, wiping her wet, brown eyes and tear-stained face. She took a deep breath and smile half-heartedly at Martha, working to pull herself together.

"If you are sure." Martha looked from one sister to the other, feeling helpless at her inability to offer comfort. Another person might offer a hug, but Martha wasn't impulsive about physical contact and was always tense in social situations. She wanted to flee, but forced herself to remain since Alegria really seemed to want her to stay.

"We will miss him. He was like a second father to us," said Veronica in heavily accented but fluent English. Sadness filled her brown eyes, but she was calmer than her sister, with tighter control over her emotions. Only her hands, gripped in front of her, suggested the shock she'd sustained.

"He was a great man, a strong man," said Alegria. She looked at Martha. "You see, my Tío Felipe, he was a fighter. Where he lives, lived, in the region of San Martin, he grew cacao for making chocolate instead of the coca for the drug dealers. At first, everyone thought the cartel would murder him, but he persuaded his neighbors to join him. They have withstood the harassment of the drug cartel for many years now. I love my uncle, my mother's brother, very much. He spent a lot of time with my sisters and me when we were children. Since he had no children of his own, he was as excited as my own parents when my son was born. Felix was like a grandchild to him."

Felix, still standing by Martha's legs, began to wail, twisting to reach a tiny hand for his mother.

"Did I do something wrong?" asked Martha.

"No. He is hungry. It's his dinner time," Alegria said as she picked the baby up and cuddled him.

"Is dinner ready?" asked Daniel. "We could all eat."

"The table is not set," said Alegria.

"I can do that while you get Felix his dinner," said Daniel.

"Can I help?" asked Martha.

"Thanks, but I've got it. You sit and relax. Talk to Veronica," he said.

Martha sank back down on the couch. Veronica sat with perfect posture, feet crossed at the ankles, in the brown, over-stuffed chair across from her.

Veronica shook her head and frowned. "I do not understand why they do not get a maid to do the cooking and cleaning. In Peru, Alegria would have a cook, a maid, and a nanny to help with the baby. She tells me that things cost more here, but can it be so much more expensive to have one maid?"

"Very few people have full-time maids or cooks here. Only the very wealthy can afford that. Cleaning services that you can hire to come weekly or monthly are available. More people use that sort of service, but most people do their own cooking and cleaning."

"In Peru, many people have maids. We haven't the same class structure as here. In Peru you are either wealthy or poor. We have few people in the middle. Of course, living there is cheaper. If Alegria moved there, she would be considered wealthy. You should come to visit Peru. The Andes are beautiful. Many tourists come to vacation there."

Martha said, "I've never thought about traveling to South America. I only know high school-level Spanish."

Veronica waved away her concern and said, "Spanish is easy compared to English. However, many Peruvians speak English, so it is not required that you speak Spanish."

A few minutes later, Daniel returned. "Dinner is ready. I didn't mean to take so long, but someone rearranged the silverware drawers and cabinets," he said, glancing at Veronica.

"Yes, I moved some things. This arrangement is more efficient. The other way did not work as well," she said with a smile.

Daniel led Veronica and Martha to a dining area just off the kitchen. The dining area was an oval, shaped by a bay window overlooking the back yard. An oak table capable of seating ten was set for three adults. Felix sat in a high chair at one end of the table with a small plate suction-cupped to his tray, eating rice, beans, and peas with his hands. A china cabinet filled one wall, with crystal goblets and platinum-rimmed china plates displayed on it.

As they ate the roasted chicken, *humitas*, and black beans with rice and salad, the phone continued to ring sporadically as relatives of Alegria called to offer condolences. Conversation flowed politely between Martha and Daniel as they discussed Peruvian food in general and the food they were eating in particular, while Alegria dealt with helping Felix eat and answering the phone calls.

Martha, who knew herself usually to be a terrible conversationalist and practically mute when tense, forced herself to follow Daniel's lead as he made an effort to carry the conversation. He seemed less distant, but still somewhat withdrawn. In spite of the lack of warmth in his eyes, Martha was grateful for his effort, slowly relaxing enough to unwind and enjoy the unfamiliar flavors of the food before her. The black beans tasted of oregano, olive oil, and garlic, adding flavor to the buttery rice. The chicken was tender and moist. The *humitas*, like moist corn patties, were flavored with onion and more garlic. Veronica hadn't added much to the conversation, but had helped feed Felix whenever he needed something while Alegria was receiving a call from yet another cousin. By the time they reached dessert, Martha finally felt the tension leave her shoulders.

Martha watched with interest as Felix attempted to feed himself. His inexpert aim caused him to miss his open mouth sometimes. Peas, rice, and beans fell down to his lap and into the convenient pocket at the bottom of his bib. Eating rice and black beans was a messy affair, as he smeared them in his hair and over every millimeter of his face. Alegria spoon-fed him mashed bits of chicken in a pudding-like consistency that Martha hadn't realized was possible for meat.

Dessert was a flan with syrupy, caramelized sugar pooling around it. The cool and creamy sweetness slid over Martha's tongue, and she savored each bite. "This flan is absolutely heavenly," she said.

"Thank you," said Alegria. "It's my grandmother's recipe."

"Could I get the recipe?" asked Martha.

"Yes, my grandmother said to share it with everyone when she gave it to me. She said she didn't understand people who kept recipes secret, since food is meant for sharing and enjoying. This way, the best recipes never die out, but get passed along and experienced by more than one family. She believed food brought people closer together, and so do I. I will make a copy for you." Alegria was standing up, with empty dishes in both hands to clear away from the table, when the doorbell rang.

Daniel jumped up. "I'll go see who's at the door."

Veronica said, "I'll clean up Felix, though I may need to bathe him to get him clean."

Martha stood and began to help clear dishes, picking up her dessert plate and spoon and following Alegria to the kitchen. The kitchen was painted pale blue with copper highlights. Copper cookware hung from an ironwork frame attached to the ceiling over the island. Painted copper plates in Peruvian llama and mountain designs decorated one wall. The switch plates and outlet covers were copper-colored. Evidence of a day spent cooking was everywhere. Pots filled the sink and stove top. Jars of herbs and spices littered the marble countertop next to the stove. Dirty spoons sat on spoon rests on the stove top. A cookbook sat open, dusted with either sugar or salt on the island next to an abandoned mixing bowl. Several white-painted cabinet doors were ajar, revealing organized canned goods and a spice rack. An empty dishwasher stood open, waiting to be filled.

"Martha, you are the guest, you don't need to help," said Alegria.

Martha was opening her mouth to respond when Daniel appeared in the doorway to the kitchen and said, "The police are here again. They want to see us. I put them in the living room." He vanished quickly, leaving Alegria frowning in confusion at the empty doorway where he had been standing.

Alegria wiped her hands on a dish towel and straightened the chocolate brown, filmy skirt she was wearing. "I wonder why they are here again," she said to Martha. "Felix didn't splatter my blouse again, did he?" she asked, gesturing to the floral-print, tailored top she wore that flattered her petite frame.

"No, you look great," said Martha. "Should I come, too?"

"Yes, I think so. If this is about Curt, you should hear it," Alegria said, still scanning her blouse for spots.

Martha followed Alegria to the living room.

Alegria spoke as she entered the room. "Hello, Detective Monroe. We were finishing a 'thank-you dinner' for Martha. Won't you sit down?" She approached and shook his hand. The massive tower of Detective Monroe dwarfed her barely five-foot height.

"Thank you," he replied, seating his oversized frame in the brown stuffed chair Veronica had occupied earlier. Martha pictured John Wayne again as she looked at him, though his deeply lined face didn't look like the deceased actor's at all. The resemblance was in his bulk and the way he moved. His khaki pants showed an ironed crease down the leg, and his button-down shirt was creased at the sleeves. His large abdomen bulged over the top of his pants, but gave more an impression of strength than blubber.

Alegria sat on the leather couch and motioned for Martha to join her. Daniel stood behind the couch, looking to Martha like a soldier at ease. All eyes rested on the detective.

Detective Monroe cleared his throat and shifted to the front of his chair, leaning forward. "As you know, Marcos Rios was caught trying to cross the border into Mexico. He is in federal custody and won't be returning to Dallas because his federal and international charges take precedence over our situation here. I sent an officer out to question him in El Paso, where he is being held. He didn't give us much information other than that an individual had hired him to do a job here. He won't define the specifics of the job."

Here Alegria interrupted. "We know the specifics! My mother called an hour ago to say that my Tío Felipe has died. He had a heart attack when a masked man delivered a letter to him saying that my Felix had been kidnapped. This happened on the day Curt was attacked, Tuesday. Tío Felipe was taken to the hospital but didn't recover consciousness before he died today."

"I see." The detective pulled out a note pad and scrawled some notes in it before looking back up. "Rios says he was given the specifics for the job here, but was paid half up front in Peru a month ago. He says the shooting was accidental. He says the gun went off during the struggle when Mr. Holliczek grabbed it. Additionally, he knew Mr. Holliczek was going to be in that parking lot that morning with the baby."

"He knew Curt's schedule that day!" said Daniel. "How?"

"It was part of the information given to him when he arrived to do the job," said Monroe.

"Curt was being followed, then?" asked Daniel.

"Rios received the information the day before the shooting, not the morning of the shooting," said Detective Monroe.

Martha looked at the detective and over her shoulder at Daniel behind her. The look on the detective's face was watchful. Daniel looked stunned.

"That would mean someone close to Curt had to feed the information to Rios." Daniel looked down at Alegria. "Who knew Curt's schedule for Tuesday?"

Alegria frowned. "I knew, Veronica knew, and I guess the people at his office knew. Did you?"

"I knew he was taking the baby with him to work for a couple hours, to show him off, because you had an appointment," Daniel said. "Did you tell anyone else, post it online, email anyone?"

"No, I don't think so," she said, shaking her head.

The detective cleared his throat. "Who is Veronica?" he asked. He held his pen in hand, poised to take more notes.

Alegria said, "My sister. She is visiting us for a few weeks. She is going through a difficult divorce in Peru, and she needed to get away from it for a few weeks. She is here now. She was going to give Felix a bath after dinner."

"Would you ask her to please come here so I can ask her some questions?" asked Detective Monroe.

"Yes, of course." Alegria stood, brushing her skirt straight as she did, and left the room.

"Now, Mr. Holliczek," said Monroe, "how long have you known your brother's wife?"

Martha watched Daniel's face. His eyelids half hooded his amber eyes, but a glint of anger came through and surprised her.

"I've known her for four years," he said.

"How long has your brother known her?" the detective asked.

Daniel's voice cut through the air. His anger was unmistakable now. "I see someone has told you that I dated her first, before Curt met her. That was a long time ago. Curt and Alegria are perfect for each other, whereas she and I are like oil and water. I irritate her because I am too blunt. Curt, on the other hand, has a silver tongue and all the tact I lack."

"How was their marriage doing? Any problems?" the detective asked.

Daniel turned a dismissive shoulder to the detective, his flash of anger cooling to a dull glow. "Ask Curt or Alegria." He paced to the door, his back to Martha and the detective, before returning to his position behind the couch with his arms crossed tightly in front of him and his fingers pressing into his biceps.

"I know that a divorce petition was filed last year and later withdrawn," said the big detective.

"Then you know they resolved their problems. Look, Alegria had post-partum depression. She could barely function. She and Curt were fighting. Their marriage was falling apart before they realized what the problem was, and she got treatment. If anything, the whole situation brought them closer together." Daniel words were rapid and angry. He paced some more before stopping and staring defiantly at the policeman, his chin up and his jaw firm around his clenched teeth.

Martha gave a slight shudder and turned back to the detective as Alegria entered the room with Veronica, who was carrying a damp-haired Felix in zipper-fronted, footed pajamas. The sweet scent of baby shampoo and baby powder drifted in like a cloud around them.

Veronica said, "You wish to speak to me?" Felix, noting his mother's presence, chose that moment to fling himself toward Alegria, reaching for her with both arms outstretched. He would have fallen if Veronica hadn't maintained a strong grip around his waist. Alegria reached over and took Felix securely under the arms, and Veronica released him.

"Yes, Ma'am. I understand you're here to visit. When did you arrive?" asked Detective Monroe.

"I came on a Monday—not this week, but the one before it."

"How long do you intend to stay?" he asked.

"Two more weeks," she said.

"You were aware that your brother-in-law was taking the baby to work with him Tuesday?" The detective sat, prepared to write on his pad, but watching her closely.

"Yes." She looked at Alegria and Daniel with one eyebrow raised, as if she found the question odd. "I knew my sister had to see the doctor that morning. I offered to keep the baby, but they had already decided Curt should take him. He was excited to show the baby off to his coworkers."

The detective looked at Alegria. "She offered to care for the baby during your appointment?"

"Yes," said Alegria.

Veronica spoke again. "I think this is the work of my husband! He is corrupt and bribes judges. He is mad at me over the divorce. Maybe he decided to kidnap the baby to get money out of Tío."

"Oh, no," Alegria said. "Surely, Roberto would not do such a thing." She looked shocked at her sister's suggestion. Alegria sank down on the couch next to Martha, cuddling her baby to her chest.

The detective asked for more information.

"His name is Roberto Aron Alvarez Diaz. I had to leave Peru because of how difficult he is making this divorce. He is a lawyer and knows many judges. I will not be treated fairly in the divorce because all the judges are on his side. He had someone following me down there. He probably has someone listening to conversations here. A device to listen would not be hard to get, would it?" she asked. Her seething anger at her husband accentuated her clipped syllables. Words rolled off her tongue in quick, harsh tones.

Detective Monroe said, "Perhaps not," and continued to scribble down notes.

"Roberto is in Dallas. He came to the house today to talk to me about dividing the business we own together. He was very angry, accusing me of ruining the business through poor investments, when he knows his failure to bill clients and collect payments on time caused the problems," Veronica said, spite and contempt marking her every word.

Martha was shaking internally with anxiety, shrinking into herself. Her arms and legs were both crossed as she sat on the couch as if to protect her body from the violence in Veronica's voice. Veronica's anger rattled her barely held together nerves. Martha realized that the man she'd seen on the lawn arguing with Veronica must have been Roberto. Had she seen the man responsible for the attacks on her and on Curt? She struggled to recall his face, but couldn't. At the time, she'd been more focused on driving than studying the couple.

"Where is he staying? Did he say?" asked the big detective.

"I don't know. He didn't tell me," she said. "But I have his phone number."

"I'd like to get that phone number, please."

Veronica yanked a phone from her pocket, jabbed at it sharply with her well-manicured finger, and then rattled off the number for him. "Roberto will call here again. He has many papers he wants me to sign."

The detective finished taking notes and looked up again.

"Mrs. Holliczek, I need to ask you some personal questions. Would you prefer to speak to me alone?" the detective asked in an even voice, looking at her with calm but intelligent gray eyes. He balanced his bulk precariously on the front edge of the stuffed brown chair. His note pad sat on his knee, and his pen floated above it in his right hand.

Martha, who had been growing more uncomfortable by the minute, jumped up from her seat on the couch, her face pale except for a creeping pink spreading through her cheeks. "I should probably go home now."

Alegria smiled gratefully at Martha. "Thank you for coming, Martha. I'm sorry our dinner wasn't as pleasant for you as I had hoped. We greatly appreciate what you did for Curt. If you hadn't been there, he would have bled to death. Thank you for saving his life." Alegria moved forward and hugged Martha, giving her a traditional Latin-American air kiss near her cheek.

Martha accepted the hug and even returned it with her one good arm. Her face was completely pink as she thanked Alegria for dinner. She'd never been the hugging type, since it felt unnatural to her. She found Alegria's gratitude embarrassing, since she didn't feel she deserved it. She glanced at Daniel.

He gave her a sheepish half grin and said, "Let me walk you out."

Veronica moved toward Martha. "I, too, would like to thank you for what you did." She also gave Martha a kiss at the air in front of her cheek and a gentle hug. Then she turned to Alegria and said, "I will put Felix to bed for you," holding her arms out to take Felix.

"Goodbye, Detective Monroe," Martha nodded to the detective as she moved quickly for the front door. Daniel beat her there, opened the door for her, and followed her out.

Chapter 10

As he closed the door with a sharp bang behind them, Daniel said, "I don't blame you for beating a hasty retreat. I want to excuse myself and go home, too, but I should stay and support Alegria. Besides, the detective seems inclined to make one of us the guilty party."

Martha looked over his shoulder at a pale-gray mockingbird launching itself from a branch of the oak in the neighbor's yard to snatch up a flittering moth. The white stripes on its wings and tail flashed. She didn't want to think anyone in the family was guilty. Her mind stuck on the fact that Curt's office had known his plans, too.

Who in the office would have any connection to a mercenary from Peru? Someone in the family then ...

"Hey!" he said sharply, recalling her attention.

Martha looked back, and Daniel's strangely colored eyes caught and held hers. That spark of anger was lit again. Martha took an involuntary step back from him, wondering again if he could see her thoughts so clearly on her face.

Daniel moved toward her. The anger left his eyes, leaving sadness behind. "We didn't do this. The detective is covering all his bases. Family is always the first place to start."

Martha could hear the insistent and persuasive, almost pleading notes in his voice. She wanted to believe him. However, nagging logic had sown a seed of doubt that was growing. She stepped away from him, and tears began to well in her eyes.

No! He saved your life!

The words cut through her brain, obliterating the doubt. She almost tripped over her own feet as she switched directions moving back toward him, her mental tug of war moving at a faster pace than her motor skills.

Daniel reached out a hand and grabbed her uninjured shoulder, steadying her inches from his chest. He slid his hand down her bare arm and took her hand in a firm grip, while his eyes looking down into hers pleaded for her trust. "We didn't do this to Curt!" he said, enunciating each word carefully and independently, trying to make her believe he was telling the truth.

Martha forced a wavering smile to her face and blinked back the threatening tears. His large hand was warm over hers and the pressure reassuring. She felt drawn to him, empathizing with his need for her to believe him. She wanted to believe him. Her throat constricted with compassion, and she had to swallow hard before she could speak. "Maybe the house was bugged, and they listened to conversations to know his schedule. Maybe Curt told someone his schedule, not realizing he was setting himself up. We'll find another explanation for how they knew where Curt would be and when," she said, trying to convince herself as much as Daniel.

Daniel released her hand and grinned at Martha with that incredibly charming, white-toothed smile. Martha couldn't have taken her eyes off him if the house had caught fire behind him. Her stomach fluttered; her heart beat faster; her breath came in a shallow gasp as she realized that she was falling for him.

I believe you. I believe you. Please be telling the truth.

"Thank you for believing me," he said. He took her hand gently and walked her to her rental car. Twice he started to say something, but changed his mind. Then, with a quick kiss to her cheek, he was gone, loping back up the drive to the front door, leaving Martha stunned but happy for the moment. The spark of warmth had returned to his eyes, but the look on his face still held a question, a hint of puzzlement. Martha thought he wanted to ask her something, but decided against asking. She wondered what he hadn't said.

BACK AT BILL's house, Martha's mind was in a whirl. She hoped Daniel would check the house for listening devices and talk to Curt about who knew his schedule. She needed a sounding board and considered laying it all out for Bill, but he and Heidi had gone to a movie and wouldn't be back until midnight, according to the note he'd left her.

She changed out of her dress into jeans and a T-shirt, pulled her hair into a thick ponytail and did her shoulder exercises. However, even the stabbing pain in her shoulder wasn't enough to turn her mind from the problem of who had hired Rios to take the baby.

After one final attempt to lift her arm, pulling against the wide, flat, green therapy rubber band that the doctor had given her, Martha gave up on her exercises for the evening. Sweat was dripping from her forehead, down her nose, and into her eyes. The muscles in her shoulder were conspiring with the ones in her neck, which had whispered something to her temples and caused them to begin to pound. Abandoning the rubber band, Martha went to the kitchen for water and pain medicine.

Standing in front of the sink in the moss-green kitchen, Martha popped the round, orange pill into her mouth. A rumbling sound like a car in the drive caught Martha's ears. Her whole body went tense. She almost choked on the pill and had to gulp water to make it go down.

No one could be at the house. It was only ten-thirty. Bill and Heidi weren't likely to be back from their movie until closer to midnight. Maybe the car was at the neighbor's house.

Barely breathing, Martha listened. Silence. Then, the knob on the door leading from the garage into the kitchen rattled.

Martha jumped back and looked around the kitchen for the phone and a weapon. Both the knife block and the telephone were on the countertop closest to the garage door. Martha darted forward to grab for them. The door knob began to turn. She altered course and skidded through the doorway into the hallway leading to her room. She slammed herself flat against the wall and peeked back around the door frame into the kitchen.

Martha's heart was pounding in her chest.

"Maybe she's gone to bed," said a familiar voice as the door swung open.

Bill came into view in his jeans and plaid shirt, pulling his keys from the doorknob. Heidi's gray head popped out from behind him and followed him into the kitchen.

Martha walked shakily back into the kitchen and sank into a chair at the round pine table. Her bare feet were cold on the stone tile floor. Relief made her legs turn to clay: heavy, yet ready to be molded into any shape rather than holding a form of their own.

"You scared me to death. I didn't expect you back this early," she said.

Heidi hurried over and looked at Martha. "Your face is as white as a sheet. Let me get you something! Would you like some herbal tea? Peppermint is a good pick-me-up. Or maybe a hot chocolate?"

"No, no thank you, Heidi. I'm fine. I don't need anything," said Martha.

"I'm sorry we scared you," Bill said as he sat at the table across from her. "We came back early because the show wasn't worth the cost of the tickets: all action and no discernible plot of any kind. I like an action movie, but it can't be one chase scene and explosion after another without an explanation of why the characters are involved in any of it. Not to mention, the characters were all clichés, and unsympathetic ones at that."

Heidi nodded her agreement and added, "By twenty minutes into the film, I was hoping the main character would get killed off so I could leave. Ten minutes later, Bill leaned over and said he wanted his money and his time back. So we got up and left."

A few minutes later, Heidi hustled Martha off to bed.

Martha slept poorly, dreaming mash-ups of hospitals, Curt morphing into a dying old man with blue lips, Daniel wearing a flat mask that he then flicked off to expose a beautiful smile and whispering something that she couldn't understand. She awoke Sunday morning feeling tired and confused and wishing she could put it all out of her mind. Fortunately, singing at church was good for clearing the mind of clutter, and she returned from church in a much more cheerful frame of mind. After that, the day flew by without pause.

Monday and Tuesday sputtered by with Martha riding to and from work with Bill and attending therapy for her shoulder in the evenings. Work was getting harder to accomplish, even as range of motion in her shoulder improved daily. Physical therapy was working wonders. The bruises turned greenish-yellow and began to fade. The insurance company's check arrived, allowing Martha to begin shopping for a car with better gas mileage and a navigation system. In a fatherly way, Bill gave her more than a few suggestions on vehicle safety.

The days would have been better if Daniel had called. Unfortunately, he hadn't. Martha decided the kiss on the cheek he'd given her had been from his adoption of the traditional South American greeting and leave-taking rituals. Her body was healing, but her brain was stuck in a jumble of confused thoughts, flashbacks to the shooting, and nightmares. Martha's shifting brain kept focusing on the problems of Curt, Daniel, and Alegria instead of on her injured workers' files. The paperwork was piling up. She was falling further behind schedule.

On Wednesday, a call in the late afternoon from Lieutenant Silk with the Carrollton Police let Martha know that her apartment was no longer a closed crime scene. His syrupy Louisiana drawl advising her that she could return home any time gave Martha reason to rejoice, which was swiftly succeeded by feelings of trepidation. She wanted to go home and be alone in her own space, but being alone might not be the safest choice.

Bill and Heidi wanted her to stay with them until the police caught Rios' associates, but she firmly and repeatedly declined, feeling she'd imposed on them for long enough and wanting time to herself in her own house. She argued that it could take weeks for the police to catch the men. Besides, with the police after them, they would probably stay in hiding instead of coming after her. In spite of her arguments, Bill relented only after she promised to set the security system that came preinstalled in her apartment and call a company to initiate monitoring of the system, which she hadn't done when she had moved into the complex. Martha collected her things and drove herself to work Thursday morning in her rental car. The day dragged on until finally Martha had to face going home.

Martha pulled into her assigned spot in her apartment complex, followed the sidewalk around the buildings and between plantings of snapdragons and rows of holly bushes, and unlocked the door to her ground-floor apartment. With determination and extreme caution, Martha walked into her apartment. She forced herself to look away from the bullet hole in the wall opposite the front door. Dwelling on what had happened the last time she had arrived home wouldn't help anything.

She surveyed her sparsely furnished front room. The blinds covering the sliding-glass door to the patio were closed, making the room look gray and shadowy from the lack of light. Martha opened the blinds to clear out the shadows. Martha's knees began to shake. She wobbled out of the entryway into the living area and sank down on the loveseat in front of the television.

Leaning back on the loveseat's dark-blue, chenille-jacquard material, Martha stared at the blank television screen, which reflected parts of the room like a dirty mirror. Three dusty bookshelves along one wall and the vertical blinds over the patio sliding-glass door stood out in the reflection. An uphol-stered rocking chair, purchased from a garage sale, sat next to the loveseat and completed the room.

What little furniture Martha had, she'd acquired second hand after she'd arrived in Dallas three months ago to start her first post-university job. Before that, she'd lived in dorms at the university, at a shared apartment with roommates, and at her parents' house. The only other items in the room were the framed pictures of her parents and family back in San Anto-nio, which stood on the mantelpiece above the faux fireplace.

The television, loveseat, and rocking chair sat as she'd left them. The bookshelves were full of her favorite books, covered with even more dust than when she'd last been home. She made a mental note to put dusting on her list of things to do. Her DVD player and music system nestled in their nook under the television. Pictures of her mom and dad sat on the mantle. Out on the patio, the potted plants were dry and wilting. She would have to water them soon, or they would die.

The air was stale, and Martha's nose detected a rotting smell in the kitchen emanating from the trash can. The kitchen was plain white with few personal touches. The counters were white laminate, the cabinets were white, and the walls were apartment-complex white. Martha didn't drink coffee, so no pot stood ready. Her few belongings all fit neatly inside the cabinets. Only the phone, the answering machine, and a roll of paper towels on a wooden holder stood on the counters. Martha had a small, wood laminate table and two mismatched chairs in the tiny dining area, purchased second hand, like the rest of her furniture. The only decorative touches she had arranged yet were the burnt-orange Texas Longhorn hand towels and pot holder set that her mother had given her, along with a set of dishes, as an apartment-warming gift. The towels hung on the oven door handle. The pot holders hung from a hook on the wall.

Since she had last been home, the salad in the refrigerator had gone bad, and her window-sill herb garden was drooping and turning brown in spots. Once she had watered the plants, cleaned out the refrigerator, and taken the trash to the dumpster, Martha ate plain spaghetti with butter and Parmesan cheese. She was out of sauces and ground beef. She mentally added grocery shopping to the to-do list.

While repeatedly telling herself to relax, her mind spinning, Martha wandered through the mundane tasks needed to get her home in order. She looked out the windows to see if she was being watched. She checked the door locks three times, and then changed her mind about the blinds, closing them all. Edgy and anxious, she felt a knot of fear tightening in her chest. Her mind kept veering off whatever task she was doing. In her distraction, half an hour after she thought she had started a load of laundry, she found that she'd loaded the machine and failed to turn it on.

Any other time, Martha would have left by now to go get groceries, in spite of the lateness of the hour. But the idea of going out after dark horrified Martha now, so she postponed grocery shopping. Bed was the only option. Sleeping in her own bed had seemed inviting, but now the ability to sleep had deserted Martha. As she lay in the dark, every possible means of attack ran through her mind, from being shot through the window to having the apartment burned down with her in it. Breath came in shallow gasps, and sweat poured off her body, dripping down her neck, rolling between her breasts and down her sides. The clock read 1:30 a.m., then 2:13, then 3:48. Martha got up and took a shower, then collapsed back on the bed at 4:15, with a towel still wrapped around her hair.

She awoke with a start, scenes of fire burning all around her searing her brain and the sound of a fire alarm ringing in her ears. The alarm clock was going off and probably had been for several minutes, and the ringing was being incorporated into her nightmare. Martha rolled over and hit the button to silence it.

Staying in bed for the day seemed like a great idea for about thirty seconds. It was Friday. She had almost made it through the week. Besides, she was getting so little done, what difference did it make if she skipped Friday? Then her brain rebelled at the idea. Her sense of responsibility wouldn't stand for such laziness.

She forced herself through her morning routine and arrived at work trembling and anxious. Walking the last block to her office building was nerve-wracking. Martha checked over her shoulder so often, she began to feel as if she'd developed a nervous tic. Her neck began to ache as if she'd pulled a muscle.

As she sat at her desk staring at the lists of items that needed to be updated before the end of the day, a desolate feeling overcame her. She didn't know where to start and she felt as if she would never finish. Previously, whenever she'd had a large amount of work to complete, she would break it down into manageable chunks, and slowly feel as if she could make progress. But even the small chunks seemed unwieldy today.

She ran her hands through her messy hair and rubbed her eyes. The monitor in front of her swam to the right and then to the left. Martha closed her eyes and blinked hard to clear her vision. It didn't work.

A feeling of lead weights descending on her shoulders and settling into the pit of her stomach forced her to put her head down on her desk. All sense of balance was gone. The world was spinning. Martha's breath came in short gasps as she realized she was not only dizzy but nauseated, and this moment felt unending, as if she was doomed to be stuck in it forever. Her heart began to pound. Heat radiated from every inch of her body. Intense pressure squeezed her chest. Breathing became harder and harder.

The world was coming to an end, and no one else had noticed.

Martha groped with one hand toward where she knew her desk phone to be. The smooth, cold plastic of the phone met her hand. She turned her head sideways on her desk and put the phone against her upturned ear. Feeling for the buttons on the phone, she entered Bill's extension.

"Bill Gelise, how may I help you?" said Bill.

"Bill, something's wrong. I can't breathe. It hurts," she whispered.

"Martha? Are you at your desk? What's wrong?"

"At my desk. Please come."

"I'm coming!"

In a moment, Bill was standing over her.

"Martha! What happened?"

"Don't know. Dizzy. Can't breathe."

"I'm calling 911."

"Okay."

An hour later, Martha found herself lying once again in a hospital bed in a cubicle-sized space with a curtain at the entrance, being evaluated. Her breathing had eased, and her chest no longer felt that it might explode from the pressure inside it.

A thirty-ish, tired-looking doctor wearing dark-blue scrubs came around the mauve curtain and stood not far from the foot of her bed.

"Hi, I'm Dr. Mikelsen. We're waiting for the results from your blood tests, but, meanwhile, I have a few questions to ask. Do you think you can answer some questions now?"

"Yes," Martha said.

"Do you have any thyroid problems?"

"I don't think so."

"Anyone in your family have thyroid problems?"

"Not that I know of."

"Do you have any heart problems?"

"No."

"What do you do for a living?"

"I'm a workers' compensation specialist."

"Is your work particularly stressful right now?"

"No."

"How long have you had this job?"

Martha could tell he was reading the questions from some sort of list. "Three months."

"Did you have to move to start your job?"

"Yes." She watched as he jotted down her answers.

"Where from?"

"San Antonio."

"Is your family there?" He looked up from his list and studied her face.

"Yes."

"Do you have any family or close friends here?"

"No."

"Has anything else been bothering you lately? Troubles with a boyfriend, maybe?" He gave her an encouraging smile. She could see he wanted a longer answer than the monosyllabic ones she'd been giving him.

"No, but I've had a crazy week or two," she said.

"Crazy in what way?"

Martha laughed and tears came to her eyes. "You wouldn't believe it all. I saw a shooting. Then, in what we think were attempts to remove me as a witness, I was almost shot at my apartment, and, a day later, I got forced into a car accident. My shoulder was injured in the car accident. The police told me to be careful and be aware of my surroundings in case I'm being followed."

"That qualifies as crazy!" The doctor paused, taking notes. He flipped to another page in the paperwork he was holding and asked another question. "Have you had trouble sleeping since the shooting?"

"Yes."

"Have you had any flashbacks to the incidents you described—the shootings or car accident?"

"I keep seeing the shooting, and I'm having nightmares," she said. He'd found another list of questions to ask her.

"Have you been avoiding the place where the shooting occurred?"

"Yes."

He made a check mark on his form and asked the next question. "Right before you felt unwell today, did you have a feeling of impending doom?"

"That question is on your list?" she asked.

He glanced up at her. "Yes. Did you have a sense of doom, like the world was ending at any moment, or like something terrible was going to happen?"

"Yes!" He made another check mark on the form he held.

"Are you having difficulty concentrating at work, too?"

"Yes."

"Well, I can tell you what's going on with you today," said the doctor, looking up from his notes. "Unless your blood tests come back to show something else, the mostly likely cause of your chest pain, difficulty breathing, and heart palpitations is stress. You've had what's sometimes called an anxiety attack or panic attack. You're also exhibiting the classic symptoms of post-traumatic stress."

"Soldiers get post-traumatic stress."

"Well, you've been shot at and seen someone shot right in front of you. You've been physically attacked and stalked in a way that would match any soldier in a war zone. On top of that, you've started a new job and moved to a new city in the last three months. New jobs and moves are two of the three main stressors for people your age. You will need to follow up with your family doctor for a referral to a psychiatrist or psychologist for therapy, or I can give you some names of people."

He flipped closed the chart in his hands and tucked it under his arm. "I've written a prescription for some medication. It will help you sleep and relieve some of your anxiety. You'll need to start with half a pill for four days, then a whole pill for four days, then one and a half for four days. After that your dose will be two pills a day. You must follow up with your doctor because you can't just stop taking this medicine. You have to slowly lower the dosage, like you slowly increase it when you start taking it. Do you understand?" He smiled at her and slid his pen into his pocket.

"Yes," she said.

"Do you have any questions?"

Martha's mind was blank. She would have dozens of questions the instant he left the room, but her brain felt numb and empty. "I can't think of anything."

Three hours later, Martha's blood test results came back negative. She signed what felt like her millionth medical form and was released.

Bill met her in the waiting area. "Can I take you home?"

"No, I don't want to ruin any more of your day than I already have. Take me back to the office. I'll catch the train home."

"I don't want to pry, but the doctors didn't find anything seriously wrong, did they?" The worry lines between his eyes were pronounced. He stood like a brick wall before her, waiting for an answer.

She laughed and tried to shrug off his concern. "The doctor diagnosed me with stress."

"Uh-huh. I could have told them that. What else?" He gave her a skeptical look. She would have to say more.

"He said I had an anxiety attack, and that I probably have post-traumatic stress." She turned to walk toward the sliding-glass doors of the exit, hoping he would follow.

"What do you need to do for treatment?" he asked the back of her head.

"I have to follow up with my doctor and get counseling."

"Did you get any prescriptions you need to fill?"

"Yes. I can take care of it." She was discomfited by his desire to help. She needed time to think about what the doctor had said. She wasn't ready to fill a prescription that might mess with her brain, especially if she couldn't simply stop taking it if she didn't like the effect it had on her. She wanted more information before she did anything. She crossed her arms in front of her. "I can't thank you enough for what you've already done for me, but please leave this to me." Her eyes began to tear up, and she was afraid the tears would spill down her cheek. She felt like a wrung-out washcloth, limp and dirty. She wanted to collapse into bed. She wanted to be left alone.

"Let me at least drive you to the train," he said. The look on his face was as stubborn as she'd ever seen him.

"Okay. Thanks."

"Quit thanking me. I'm here to help," he said, giving her a fleeting smile that didn't erase the worry in his eyes.

ARRIVING HOME THIRTY minutes later, Martha took the prescription out of her purse and stared at it. She didn't want to fill it. She'd seen enough commercials for anxiety and antidepressant medications to know that they all came with side effects. She sat down at her laptop and searched for information on the medication. The articles she read did nothing to make her want to take the medication. Some of the known side effects were severe. Even the thought of taking the pills now made her feel ill, anxious.

She reasoned that the problem was only stress, and warranted, logical stress at that. People were trying to kill her. That would make anyone anxious and would give anyone nightmares and problems sleeping. She'd dealt with stress before, and she would deal with it now. Anyway, the police would catch Rios' associates. The situation would be resolved, and her anxiety would go away. She didn't need to medicate herself out of it. Besides that, she'd read that antidepressants didn't work for a lot of people anyway. What she needed was exercise. That always helped her relax. Martha slid the prescription into her desk drawer, not realizing that her anxiety had reached a level where it was disrupting her logical thought processes.

Chapter 11

After a long, sleepless night, Saturday morning dawned. Martha pulled on a pair of yoga pants and an old college T-shirt she'd gotten free for giving blood. She headed to the apartment complex's workout room with the intention of spending at least an hour on the various machines and doing her shoulder exercises, in spite of how tired she felt.

Returning to her apartment an hour and a half later, sweaty and thirsty, Martha walked to the bare white kitchen for a drink of water. The blinking light on her phone caught her eye. She listened to the message as she filled her cup from the water dispenser on the refrigerator door.

Alegria's voice filled her head. "Martha, this is Alegria. The doctors released Curt from the hospital Thursday, and he wants to meet you. Will you be free to join us at a restaurant Wednesday evening? Please call me back."

As the message clicked off, Martha pictured Curt's face. Then, all her brain could recall was the blood oozing through her balled-up sweater and covering her hands. The smell of iron hit her nostrils. A wave of nausea swept through her. Martha ran to the sink and heaved convulsively, but managed not to throw up.

You can't see him again. You can't see him again. You can't do it.

Yes, I can. He wants to meet me, and I will go to dinner!

The rest of the day passed in an exhausted blur of grocery shopping and house cleaning: dinner of a bowl of cereal, some nonsensical comedy on television that didn't seem at all funny, and bedtime.

The blaring sound of an alarm going off almost startled Martha off her bed. She was instantly awake with her heart in her throat as she realized it wasn't the fire alarm but her security system wailing at an eardrum-rupturing level. The clock glowed red numbers: 1:15 a.m. Martha leaped from her bed to the control panel on the wall by the door to her bedroom. The flashing light indicated that someone had tried to open the sliding-glass door to the patio. Martha locked her bedroom door as the phone began to ring. Snatching up the phone and panting slightly, she said, "Hello?"

"This is Redding Security Systems. Is there an emergency?" said a male voice.

"I don't know. I haven't gone to see if someone tried to come in or not," Martha said.

The door knob to Martha's room shook.

"Someone's inside! Send the police!" she yelled urgently into the phone as she launched herself into her closet and pulled the door until it was barely ajar. Dropping the phone to the floor, Martha knocked all the clothes off the short pole on which they'd been hanging. Blouses and skirts landed in a jumble of hangers at her feet. She wrenched the pole out of the metal sockets that secured it between the wall and a built-in shelving unit. Gripping the three-foot pole like a baseball bat, Martha peeked out the crack between the door and door frame. Standing in a matching pink shorts-and-top pajama set with her heavy, brown hair tumbling into her face, Martha shivered.

The hairs on her neck stood up as something banged against her bedroom door, shaking it in its frame. She could hear a voice calling to her from the phone at her feet, but she couldn't make out the words over the alarm that was still blaring, despite its being muffled slightly by the closet door. As she watched, her bedroom door came crashing open. A short, chubby man in dark pants and shirt with a red bandana covering his nose and mouth dodged into the room. He held a gun out before him, swinging it in an arc, scanning for his target.

Martha saw the man's eyes spy the master bathroom door. It was closed. He approached it swiftly and kicked it open. Martha considered trying to run for the hallway while he checked the bathroom, but he didn't enter it. Instead, he stood in the doorway and flicked on the light. He realized instantly that she wasn't there and turned back to the bedroom. The man zeroed in on the closet door, bounding toward it sideways, with his held sideways, gangster-style. He stopped and tried to nudge the door open with the muzzle of the gun.

Her heart slamming in her chest, Martha shoved the door open as hard as she could with her foot. The door's edge flattened the man's nose. The gun went off with a deafening boom almost next to Martha's ear. Martha swung the pole at the gun. The man, holding his nose with one hand, yelped as the pole slammed into his forearm. The gun popped out of his hand. Martha swung the pole repeatedly, bringing it down on the man's head and shoulders. He ducked down, putting his arms over his head to protect himself from the blows, then turned and fled the room.

Martha ran to the door through which the man had fled and paused, readying the pole to swing again, before peeking down the hall leading to her living room. The shifting shadows and darkness of the hallway revealed nothing. Martha couldn't see whether the man had left or not. The alarm was still blaring, but sounded muffled to ears still reverberating with the sound of a gun going off. Afraid to turn the lights on in case the man had an armed accomplice, Martha slid forward in the dark. She inched slowly into the hallway and saw two men with flashlights appear in the living room in front of her. The alarm was suddenly silenced.

"Police! Is anyone here?" said one of the men.

Martha lowered the rod, her blood pounding in her ears, and responded, "I'm back here! Did you catch him? Is he gone?"

One officer trained a flashlight on Martha. "Drop the bat!" he ordered.

Martha dropped the rod and realized her injured shoulder was throbbing.

"Walk forward with your hands up in front of you!"

Martha did as she was told, stopping in the living room in front of the loveseat.

"Are you the owner of this property? Do you live here?" the officer barked.

"Yes, I live here!"

"We apprehended a man fleeing the apartment. Are you injured?"

"I'm okay. He had a gun. I knocked it out of his hand with the rod. It's in my room somewhere." Martha's whole body began to tremble. Her knees gave out, and she fell down on the loveseat.

More officers came into the apartment, some from the broken sliding-glass door, sitting open, and some through the front door. A few disappeared into Martha's room. Someone draped a blanket around Martha's shoulders.

Martha was exhausted, barely focusing on the officers who came in and out of her range of vision and moved around the periphery. She felt detached from them all, as if she was watching from a distance instead of from a few feet away.

An officer sat in front of her and asked again if she was injured.

"No, I'm not. My shoulder hurts, but that's from before. You should get Lieutenant Silk. He'll know what's going on."

"Lieutenant Silk?" the unknown officer said.

"Yes, I'm sure this is related to the last two attempts to kill me."

"Two attempts ... This is the third time someone has tried to kill you?" the officer asked.

Martha was too tired to go through it all again. She laid her head down on the arm of the loveseat and repeated, "Get Lieutenant Silk," before closing her eyes and putting her arm over her face. She didn't even have the energy left to be upset or mad. Her emotions had evaporated. She began to drift into unconsciousness.

A while later, Martha heard a voice calling her name as a hand gently shook her shoulder. She sat up, more alert now, and looked for a clock to tell her what time it was.

Lieutenant Silk knelt in front of her, blocking her view of the clock on the DVD player. Martha focused on him, noting his damp blonde hair and the fresh smell of soap, and asked, "What time is it?"

His lips creased into a small smile, and he glanced at his watch. "It's two a.m."

"I wasn't out that long then. I feel better now, though," Martha said. "Sorry to get you out of bed, but I didn't want to have to explain everything all over."

His blue eyes flashed understanding. His Louisiana accent seemed stronger in the middle of the night. "You didn't get me up. My two-month-old son did that. Ah guess ah was wrong when ah said you could come home. Sorry 'bout that. If it helps, we caught two men tonight: the one who came in and one who was waiting for him. They match the description of the men who caused the car accident. We'll need you to identify them if you can. Can you answer some questions?"

"Yes. I know. You need a statement. I'm getting pretty good at giving those." She brushed her brown hair back out of her face and remembered she was still in her pajamas. Luckily, she'd chosen the pink short set instead of an oversized T-shirt or short nightgown. "Can we do it here? If we have to go to the station, I want to get dressed first."

"We can start here, but first, is there someone we can call for you?"

"No, I don't want to bother anyone at two a.m."

"By the way, what'd you do to the suspect? He's got two black eyes, a broken nose, and a lump the size of an egg on his forehead," he said.

"I hit him with the door first. Then I hit him with the rod that the clothes hang on in the closet. I hope I did some damage. He had a gun."

"We found it by the bed. It's been collected into evidence," he said. "You did a good job tonight. You should be proud of yourself."

"Adrenalin is amazing stuff, but if I have another couple weeks like this, I'm going to end up an adrenalin junkie. Then, I'll have to go looking for excitement, maybe take up skydiving."

Lieutenant Silk grinned widely at her and shook his head. "Will you come identify the suspects for us now? Then, let's get the paperwork outta the way." He wore a windbreaker jacket labeled Carrollton Police Department with the city emblem on the front left breast over a pair of black slacks. The jacket rustled as he moved. He hopped lightly up from his knees and reached down a hand to her.

Martha grabbed his warm, strong hand and stood up. She dropped the blanket on the couch. "Okay," she said. "Let's do this."

A few hours later, Martha sat in a booth at a café for breakfast. The café's style was farmhouse kitsch. Shelving sprouting every conceivable kind of patchwork rooster or ceramic pig surrounded the red-and-white checkered tables. An antique butter churn stood in one corner with silk flowers erupting from it. The cheery, cozy atmosphere appealed to Martha, a stark contrast to her own apartment, which was now crawling with police.

It was only six-thirty in the morning. Still too early to call Bill and Heidi and ask to come over. At least it was Sunday. Martha decided to go to early church services before she called Bill. Lieutenant Silk said her apartment would be a crime scene for the rest of the day and maybe until Monday. She'd have to ask to use Dora's room again. She'd packed a suitcase and tossed it into her car before the police escorted her out of her apartment.

A waitress in a blue gingham dress and frilly pocketed apron delivered her order and vanished, leaving Martha to her thoughts. Her mind flooded with relief. The police had confirmed that the men caught at her apartment were the same ones that had caused the accident. They were even using the same car. The men confessed that Rios had hired them, although they claimed that they had only meant to scare her, not kill her. Martha could only identify the man who had broken into her bedroom. When the police had shown him to her in the parking lot of her apartment, he'd looked away, not meeting her eyes. His nose was still dripping blood, and the purple-and-black bruising around his swollen eyes was still forming. The police made him remove an ice pack from his forehead when she came out to identify him. He deserved to feel every bruise and bump.

If only she weren't worried about who had hired Rios initially, Martha would have been able to empty her mind and consume her omelet in perfect contentment. She wanted to believe that someone in Peru intent on extorting money from

Alegria's uncle had planned the attack on Curt. Perhaps it had been Veronica's soon-to-be ex-husband. She wanted to believe he had paid someone to follow the Holliczek family and listen in on conversations to learn the best time to try to kidnap the baby. She wanted to believe that Daniel, Alegria, and Veronica weren't involved. Still, the logic centers in her brain weren't willing to eliminate them as suspects.

FOUR HOURS LATER Martha blinked herself awake and remembered where she was as her eyes fell on the posters and trophy shelf on the wall. Panic that had started to rise as consciousness returned abated. She felt safe here. Martha had arrived at the Gelises' home shortly after church. Heidi had escorted her straight to Dora's room and told her to get some rest. Her ringing cell phone awakened her from a thankfully dreamless sleep, but stopped ringing before she could get to it. Rubbing her achy shoulder, Martha reached for her phone and listened to the voicemail message.

"Hello, Martha, this is Alegria. Curt would like to meet you. In my last message, I know I said Wednesday for dinner, but Curt doesn't want to wait that long. Could you come for dinner at Georgio's Italian Restaurant on Beltline in Addison, on Monday evening at seven o'clock? I know it's short notice. Please call me back."

The message ended. Going to dinner with Curt and Alegria would mean seeing Daniel, and probably Veronica and little Felix, too. So many people would mean a lot of conversation and would require a staggering amount of energy. Martha felt too drained to even consider it. She dropped the phone back on the night stand and sank back down on the floral-patterned pillow that matched the sheets and bedspread on the bed.

A gentle knock sounded at the door. Martha sprang back up and sat on the edge of the bed before calling, "Come in."

Heidi peeked into the room. "How are you feeling? I heard your phone ring and thought you might want a drink or something to eat. Can I get you anything?"

"I'm getting up. I feel much better now that I've had some sleep. I'll come out to the kitchen and get a drink." Martha hopped up off the bed, trying to appear perky. She didn't want Heidi to worry about her. "I'll be down there in a minute. Let me fix my hair."

Heidi nodded and vanished behind the closed the door.

Surveying her crumpled blouse and flyaway hair, Martha set about improving her appearance. She brushed out her brown hair and pulled it back into a smooth ponytail and put on mascara to make her eyes look at little more vibrant than she was feeling. Finally, she put on a clean, unwrinkled T-shirt before walking down to the kitchen.

As they settled around the kitchen table in the now-familiar, moss-colored kitchen, the motherly, solicitous, and always active Heidi hovered over Martha. Today, she wore a pale-yellow blouse over blue walking shorts that exposed her freckled legs. Her bare feet tapped the floor beneath her when she finally sat down across from Martha.

Martha gulped a glass of iced Dr. Pepper and felt it burn her throat as she swallowed. She needed a caffeine kick.

"Since the police caught those men last night, is your trouble over? They have everyone who attacked you, don't they?"

"I think so. Someone hired Rios to try to kidnap the Holliczeks' baby. That person knew Curt's schedule and where he would be, but that may have been from listening in on conversations, bugging the house, or hacking his phone. Whoever started all this hasn't been caught."

"That doesn't have anything to do with you, right? You aren't involved in that part?"

"I think I should be okay, especially if the mastermind for all this is in Peru or if it's Alegria's sister's husband, Roberto. The police are already looking at him as a suspect. Alegria Holliczek invited me to dinner Monday. Her husband, Curt, is out of the hospital and wants to meet me." Martha interlaced her fingers on the pine table to keep from drumming them or twiddling them.

"Bill said the police advised you not to associate with the family. Are you going to ignore that advice?"

Martha looked at Heidi's face, which was full of concern. "Daniel Holliczek saved my life. I don't believe that he or Alegria had anything to do with the attack on Curt. They've both been incredibly kind to me. Alegria's uncle had problems with the drug cartels in Peru. He refused to give in to them. He had received a note saying Alegria and Curt's baby had been kidnapped, and demanding ransom money. He was so upset that he had a heart attack and died. The people behind all of this are probably in Peru."

"Maybe if the uncle is dead, they won't continue to attack Alegria's family, provided she didn't inherit from him," Heidi said. "Do you know who inherits? We don't know how determined these people are. They might change tactics to extort money from whoever inherits." Heidi leaned her chin on her fist, still frowning.

"Wouldn't it be easier for them to choose a different target? Finding out who inherits and targeting them feels like it would require a mafia vendetta or a blood feud, which seems like something from another century. If the uncle was the target, they've killed him. What more could they do to him? I can't see this continuing."

"So, you're going to dinner Monday?"

Martha realized she'd talked herself into going to dinner while she'd tried to convince Heidi it was safe. She should go. She did want to meet Curt and talk to him. Maybe seeing him up and alive would erase the visions she kept having of him bleeding in the parking lot. "Yes, I'm going to dinner Monday."

She finished her Dr. Pepper, pulled out her phone, and left a message for Alegria saying she would meet them at the Italian restaurant on Monday.

Sunday afternoon, Martha returned her rental car and went car shopping with Bill, who was apparently enjoying treating Martha like a foster daughter whom he could advise on the purchase of a new vehicle. They started at a large used-car lot franchise. Martha's innate frugality rebelled at the thought of buying a brand-new car that would devalue the instant she left the lot. Her parents had always purchased nearly new, low-mileage cars. They'd taught her to save money where she could. Getting a newer-model used car with a good warranty was the budget-saving lesson her father had taught her when she'd bought her first car. She wished he could be with her shopping now, but Bill made a good surrogate.

She'd loved her Ford Focus, and this time she selected a low-mileage, newer-model Ford Fusion. The car came with a navigation system, and she could use Bluetooth to sync her telephone to its speaker system. The blue-black paint color was darker than Martha wanted, since darker colors heated up faster in the hot summer sun. However, the leather seats inside were a pale gray, which she hoped wouldn't get hot enough to burn her rear end when she sat on it. Bill approved of the car's safety features, but couldn't help expressing his concern about the size of the vehicle.

"Are you sure you don't want something larger? Smaller cars always come out the losers in crashes. With so many bigger vehicles on the road, you need a bigger vehicle to protect yourself."

"Bill, this car has good safety features. I'm not buying an SUV or a pickup truck just because everyone else has one. I don't need a big vehicle. Besides, this one gets great gas mileage. With the price of gas going up like it is, I'd do better with the smaller car."

"Well, I agree with you on the economics of your choice. But still ..."

"I won't have people trying to chase me down and kill me for the rest of my life. The police have caught all my stalkers. I need a car that works for me next year, not only for right now."

Bill gave her a reluctant smile and graciously surrendered. He waited patiently in the lobby while the salesman and Martha completed the paperwork, and then followed her back to his house as she drove her new car.

MONDAY MORNING, MARTHA rode to work with Bill after Martha failed to convince him that it was her turn to drive him. Bill checked his rearview mirrors frequently and insisted that Martha not go to lunch alone. She couldn't convince him that her attackers were all behind bars.

Martha looked forward to dinner. Every time her mind wandered from her work and her brain produced an image of flowing blood, she tried to picture Curt happily eating dinner. Work still seemed impossible, but Martha kept plugging away at each day's required pieces. She got the bare minimum done. A call from Lieutenant Silk with information about the men who'd broken into her apartment provided a late-afternoon distraction.

At the end of the day, Bill came to Martha's desk to see if she was ready to leave. He found her logged out of her computer, purse in hand, phone to ear.

"Yes, Alegria, I'll see you tonight. Bye," she said into the phone.

"Are you sure you want to be involved with them?" said Bill.

"We've discussed this already, Bill. I don't believe they're involved. I'm not in danger anymore. The people responsible for all the trouble are probably in Peru." Martha fought to control her temper and to keep tears from welling up. She felt like every conversation caused her to have an overly emotional response.

Stop it, control yourself, and be polite! Bill doesn't deserve this snippy attitude!

"What about the man you saw downtown with Rios? Did they identify him?"

"The police think he's one of the men who came to my apartment. Lieutenant Silk called this afternoon. He said one of the men caught at my apartment is named Jesse Hernandez and works in a building near the Chinese restaurant downtown. He said Hernandez is the man from the video in the tunnels. I haven't seen him yet, since he's not the guy who came into my apartment, but I'm sure Lieutenant Silk wouldn't say it if he wasn't positive." Martha knew Bill was concerned for her safety, but he could be exasperating.

"Okay, then, I'll say no more about it. Enjoy your dinner." He flashed her a big smile and changed the subject. "Are you ready to go?"

"Yes." She stood and followed Bill to the elevators.

The momentary annoyance with Bill evaporated, leaving behind guilt for making him worry about her. Seeing Curt would be good for her, Martha reasoned. If she could see him up and moving and happy, maybe she could erase the memories of him bleeding. She was also looking forward to seeing Daniel, although she wasn't thrilled with the social situation she'd be in. Sitting and eating with people required conversation. She'd have to make an effort not to look as anxious and worn out as she felt.

Chapter 12

Georgio's Italian restaurant on Beltline Road in Addison wasn't hard to find. It was housed in a small building painted a warm Tuscan yellow and decorated with heavy ceramic-tiled pots overflowing with herbs and flowers lining paths to a faux courtyard at the entrance, making it an oasis in the heat. Two sides of the building provided a light fog of cool mist from misting stations installed in the roof. Having arrived twenty minutes early, Martha elected to wait inside the restaurant.

Settling on a hard sofa in a waiting-area nook, Martha tried to read but found she couldn't focus on the pages. She looked up at the door every thirty seconds to watch for approaching people or to see who was coming inside. Finally, she abandoned the book and stared at the door until at last she saw Daniel pull it open. He stood back and allowed Alegria to walk in with Curt, who looked nothing like Martha's memory of him. The intense pain was gone from his face.

Alegria saw Martha and came forward to hug and air kiss her on the cheek. "Martha, I hope we did not keep you waiting. It's good to see you again."

Curt came forward with his hand outstretched. "Martha, I'm pleased to finally meet you again."

Martha took his hand, which was large, square, and warm. She noted his eyes were an ordinary dark brown but set in his face under eyebrows that reminded her of Daniel's. "I'm happy to see you doing so well. I'm amazed you're up and around already. Should you be out walking like this?"

"The hospital released me with instructions to care for the wound and to avoid tearing my stitches. That doesn't mean I have to lie in bed all day. I'm going to walk in spite of everyone treating me like an invalid. I keep telling them if I sit around I'll lose muscle mass and strength." He grinned at her, and his face lit with good humor and charm that also mirrored Daniel's.

"He is stubborn as a mule!" said Alegria, forcing a frown on her lips but with a smile in her eyes. "He will not rest. I had to convince him not to mow the lawn yesterday."

"The mower is self-propelled. I wouldn't have hurt anything," Curt said. "Anyway, I was kidding. I wouldn't have done it."

"Of course, you wouldn't. I wouldn't have let you," she said.

Curt and Daniel both laughed out loud.

Though clearly related, Curt and Daniel weren't all that much alike. Curt was average height, maybe five feet ten inches and stocky, with wide shoulders and a barrel chest. Daniel was two inches taller and leaner, with a runner's lack of body fat. Where Curt gave the impression of compact strength, Daniel was long and wiry. Daniel was casual in jeans, boots, and a polo shirt. Curt wore ironed khaki slacks and a button-down shirt over leather, lace-up shoes.

"Where is Felix?" Martha said.

"Veronica volunteered to watch him so that we could have a quiet night out. He can be difficult in restaurants," said Alegria. Her stylish knit dress hugged her petite frame, emphasizing her tiny waist and round hips. She had twisted her long dark hair up on her head with the ends coming loose and cascading down in back.

A black-clad hostess came and led them to a booth, where Alegria sat on one side with Curt, and Daniel slid in next to

Martha. A conventional still life of apples and pears in a bowl hung on the wall by the table. Fake, battery-operated tea-light candles flickered in the center of the white tablecloth.

After they had placed their drink orders, Martha glanced up to catch Daniel's eyes on her face. They flashed back to his brother across from him.

The drinks arrived and the waitress took their meal orders: steak florentine for Daniel, sausage and mushroom pasta for Curt, Tuscan soup for Alegria, and chicken marsala for Martha.

As the waitress left, Curt raised his glass. "A toast to you, Martha, for saving my life. If you ever need anything, let me know. I owe you a great deal."

"No, you don't. We're even. Daniel saved my life the same day I saved yours, so he discharged the family debt."

"Daniel doesn't get to discharge my debts. Right, Daniel?"

"Don't pull me into this," said Daniel.

"If he can't discharge your debt, then I owe him as much as you owe me, and I could never hope to repay him." Martha avoided Daniel's amber eyes as she spoke, keeping focused on Curt. "Please, let us be even."

Curt laughed again, a robust laugh with his mouth open wide and his slightly crooked lower teeth showing.

"All right, if that's what you want, we'll call it even. I'll toast you, and you can toast Daniel."

They all raised their glasses, clinked them together, and then drank.

"How have you been, Martha? I called Detective Monroe yesterday to see if he had learned anything new, and he told me that some men were apprehended breaking into your apartment. That must have been scary," said Alegria.

Daniel jerked his head around toward Martha and back to Alegria. "What's this? You didn't tell me!"

"The men who caused the car accident came back. My alarm system went off when one of them jimmied the sliding-glass door on my patio. Luckily, the alarm company sent the police. They arrested both the man who broke into my apartment and his accomplice, who was waiting in the car." A vision of the bandana-faced man swinging his gun toward her flashed through Martha's mind, and she shuddered slightly.

"That's not all, is it?" asked Daniel. "What happened when the man came into your apartment?"

Martha looked at him, and her eyes fixed on the amber again. She was completely aware of how close he was sitting to her. "I locked my bedroom door and hid in the closet. He broke through the door and came looking for me with a gun."

Alegria gasped. "Oh, no!"

"Then what?" asked Daniel.

"I took the clothing rod off the wall in the closet. When he got close to the closet, I slammed the door into his face and hit the gun out of his hand with the rod. Then, I kept hitting him until he ran away, straight into the arms of the police. The policeman told me I gave him two black eyes, a broken nose, and a lump on the head."

"Good for you!" said Curt.

"How lucky he didn't shoot you!" said Alegria.

"That *was* lucky. The gun fired when I hit him with the door, but he missed me."

"So, after you saved me, a man tried to shoot you at your apartment. Then, he sent two other guys to try and kill you, and they caused a car accident. Since you survived that with only an injured shoulder, they came back, broke into your apartment, and tried to kill you again. I still owe you! All that happened because you saved me," said Curt.

"No, let's not start that again. I'm glad that the people involved have been caught. I wish I knew what started all this. Do you still think it was some drug lord trying to extort money from your uncle?" Martha asked.

"As far as we can figure out, that seems to be it," said Daniel.

"Then, now that he's dead, it should be over?" Martha asked hopefully. "The cartel hired Rios, who hired the other two. Now they're in jail."

"I hope it's over. Are you allowed back home now?" asked Curt.

"Yes, I plan to go home tonight after dinner."

"Have you been in a hotel again or with friends?" asked Alegria.

"I went back to Bill and Heidi's house. They've been absolutely wonderful to me. I don't know what I'd have done without them."

"Bill is your manager at work? Is Heidi his wife?" Alegria asked.

Martha felt Daniel suddenly go still next to her. His eyes were on her face, but she forced herself to keep looking at Alegria. "Yes. Bill and Heidi's daughter is away at college, so they let me stay in her room."

"I didn't realize your manager was married when you said you were staying with him," said Alegria. "I thought perhaps he was a special friend of yours." Her eyes slid from Martha to Daniel's face and back again.

Martha laughed and turned red.

That's why he didn't call.

She risked looking at Daniel, only to find him looking sheepish with an odd, twisted smile on his face.

The words *"Yes, sorry"* floated into Martha's brain, although Daniel was now looking at Curt and Alegria. He didn't look at Martha.

He's reading my mind again.

"Yes, I am. Sorry about that."

Martha felt off balance on the padded bench of the booth. Had he answered her thoughts? She looked frantically around at the others at the table to see if they had noticed anything. She looked at Alegria, who was digging for something in her purse, unaware that anything unusual might have happened. When Martha glanced at Curt, she found that he was watching her with interest.

"Is something wrong? Curt asked.

Martha started to answer him with a denial, but couldn't do it. She turned to Daniel and said, "You're in my head. Why do I hear you in my head?"

"You can hear me?" Daniel asked, astonished. He looked from her to Curt, who grinned at him, and back again.

Curt said to Daniel, "I told you that would get you in trouble someday." He turned to Martha. "He's doing his thing again, isn't he? It's disconcerting at first, but you get used to it. He answered a question you didn't ask, didn't he? He's been doing that since I was eight, and he was five years old. Mostly, he hears other people, but they can't hear him. I've been telling him that, someday, someone other than his siblings was going to hear him. Then he'd get a shock. Now he finally has!"

Alegria looked up and frowned at Daniel. "How many times have I told you not to listen to people's thoughts? If I catch you in my head, you will regret it!" She turned to Martha. "The good news is that he has to be within a few feet of you to do this trick of his."

That they weren't teasing was apparent. Digesting the information took a second. "When you saved me at the apartment, you said you'd honed your reflexes in Iraq. Did you hear him thinking? Is that how you knew Rios was in my apartment, waiting to shoot me?"

"Yes. I was slow that time, too. I was so busy talking to you that I didn't hear him until you started to open the door. By that point in Iraq, I would have been too late."

"I see. How? Do you hear words? See pictures?"

"Both. How, I have no idea. I was born with it. It was sharp while I was in Iraq, though. There, I needed it to save my life, so I was probably focused on using it more than I am here. Here, it's an invasion of privacy, so I do try hard not to listen to anyone who walks near me. Not to mention, most people are pretty boring in their thoughts. It can be distracting, too, if I want to think about something else, and other people's thoughts keep intruding."

"Can you block them out, then?" asked Martha.

"Keeping ear buds in with music or podcasts helps, but that won't block someone who is particularly emotional, either happy or disturbed. They're louder, for some reason. Usually, I try to maintain a distance between me and other people, if I don't want to hear them think."

"How close do you have to be for you to hear people think?"

"Usually within a couple of feet. Though, in Iraq, I could extend it. Close proximity is necessary."

"I heard you all the way across the parking lot at the Colombian restaurant after you saved me from the gunman in my apartment."

"You heard me? You didn't say anything."

"I thought I imagined it. I didn't know you had special super powers!"

Daniel smiled and shook his head, and his voice took on a teasing note. "I don't have super powers. Maybe you do, if you can hear my thoughts."

"I've never heard anything else, though, whereas you, apparently, do all the time. And, that was all the way across a parking lot, not close up."

"Okay, I can project comments farther than I can hear other people, for some reason. Though, until now, no one has ever heard me respond to them, except my brother and sister."

Both Alegria and Curt watched their exchange with interest. The married couple then passed a look between them that clearly meant something significant.

"Now don't you two start on me!" said Daniel.

"What?" asked Martha.

"Sorry, but their thoughts are pretty loud right now," said Daniel.

Curt took up the conversation, changing the subject, "Veronica's husband, Roberto, came by the house to see her today. He didn't arrive in the country until after I got shot. Veronica still thinks he could have planned it. I think he was genuinely upset when I told him about Alegria's uncle dying. His family is from the same town as Alegria and Veronica, so his parents went to school with their uncle. In small towns like that, everyone knows everyone."

"So you think she's wrong to blame him?" asked Martha, forcing herself to listen to Curt.

"She'd like to blame him for causing everything from the Kennedy assassination to Hurricane Katrina, if she could. I've always found him to be friendly and generous. People can fool anyone if they try, though, so I can't say I'm a hundred percent positive he didn't organize the attack on me."

The waitress arrived with the food, which was hot and delicious. The conversation turned to Curt's recovery and continued treatments, and then to Martha's therapy. Martha told them about her new car, which Daniel expressed interest in seeing after dinner. Daniel and Curt discussed work, what Daniel was doing, and what Curt would miss. Alegria felt he should stay home longer than he intended. Martha could see a spirited battle brewing on that subject.

Dinner ended too soon for Martha. That it could be nine-thirty already seemed impossible. The restaurant was emptying. An employee was vacuuming the adjacent room. The bill was paid, with Martha's portion covered by Curt and Alegria after a short argument that Martha lost. Martha realized that she'd never win an argument with Curt. He had a debater's arguing skills coupled with enough charm to sell anyone anything, but he handled her in a way that showed he respected her position and wanted her to be comfortable with the final decision. She could see why Daniel had called him silver-tongued.

Curt and Alegria had parked by the door. Alegria went to the driver's door, in spite of Curt's protests that he was capable of driving. She was used to his debating abilities and countered them by refusing to listen.

"No! You are not driving! I will not let you convince me that you can! Get in the car," she said, with one hand on her hip and the other pointing at the car. Curt laughed and did as he was told.

Martha lingered next to Daniel, watching the car back out of the parking spot. She was glad she'd promised to show him her car. She wasn't ready to give up his company. The restaurant's patio was scented with herbs and flowers. The breeze swirled the mixture of fragrances through the warm air around them. The misting fog from above settled on her face and arms, cooling her skin. The evening light was dark gray, the sky a deep purple. Decorative globe-covered lights on poles lit the patio around the door to the restaurant.

Something shimmered in the light on the ground, catching Martha's eyes. A liquid was puddled where Curt and Alegria's car had been parked. The car must be leaking oil. They should have that checked.

Daniel turned suddenly and looked at her and at where she was looking.

The word "STOP!" reverberated through the night air and ricocheted through Martha's head. She stared at Daniel, unsure whether he had actually yelled or it was only in her head.

Across the parking lot, the car jerked to a stop as Alegria slammed on its brakes. Daniel ran toward the car as Alegria put it in park. Curt got out and waited for Daniel to reach him.

A second later, Martha ran after him, not knowing why. The hair on the back of her neck stood up and goose bumps covered her arms in spite of the evening heat. Something was wrong.

"You're leaking something. It doesn't look like oil, so it could be coolant or power-steering fluid," said Daniel.

They stood aside as Alegria reversed the car into the nearest parking space, turned the engine off, and popped the hood.

Daniel retrieved a flashlight from his truck and joined Curt at the front of the car. Martha joined Alegria next to them.

After a quick glance under the car, Daniel moved the light around the engine slowly until he located the power-steering fluid. The beam illuminated the reservoir and spotlighted a small round puncture in the side of it. Fluid had already leaked down to the level of the puncture. It would continue to slosh out when the car was in motion or on an uneven surface.

Curt drew in a sharp breath and followed it with a single word: "Damn."

"Someone punched a hole in the power-steering fluid reservoir. Your power steering could have given out completely while you were driving," said Daniel.

"What does that mean?" asked Alegria.

"We could have lost control of the car. If it happened on a turn, we could have ended up going into oncoming traffic or slamming into something," said Curt.

"Someone did this on purpose?" she asked, her voice pitched higher than usual. Martha could sense that Alegria was trembling next to her, although she couldn't see her well in the dim shadows.

"Yes," said Curt. "Someone is trying to kill me or us. We need to call the police again."

"Oh no," said Martha. "We're in Addison."

"So what?" asked Daniel. He and Curt gave her puzzled looks. She could barely see their matching eyebrows drawn together over different noses.

"That means a third police department. If this was Carrollton, we could call Lieutenant Silk. If it was Dallas, we'd get Detective Monroe. Now we have to go over the whole thing from the start again with *another* police department."

Daniel laughed, his eyes lighting up. "Someone tried to kill them, and your main concern is having to deal with another police department?"

"Well, if you put it that way, I guess it isn't that big a deal." She smiled with effort, suddenly exhausted again. "I'm tired of making formal statements to the police. The important questions are, who did this and when, and why. Could it have happened while we were in the restaurant?"

Curt answered her after scanning the parking area. "I don't think so. We were parked facing the windows right by the front door. Someone had to open the hood and slam a screw driver or something into the reservoir. People would notice that. Not to mention, the restaurant has security cameras." Curt pointed to cameras mounted on the building and onto the tops of light posts in the parking lot.

"If you get home and find a lot of fluid in your driveway, you'll know it probably happened there," said Daniel. "Y'all live in Dallas. You could call Detective Monroe, and let him deal with Addison PD. Has anyone been around your house lately? Any visitors?"

"Veronica is still there, and Roberto came to see her today. She hasn't been answering his calls, so he came looking for her. I think he's frustrated with her refusal to discuss splitting their business," said Curt. "I haven't seen anyone hanging around the neighborhood, but I haven't been watching for anyone, either."

"You've had the car parked openly in the driveway?" asked Daniel.

"Yes. The car is usually in the driveway in front of the house. Let's leave the car here for the night. Daniel can give us a ride home," said Alegria. Her voice shook.

Curt walked over and put an arm around his wife. "We'll figure this out, Sweetie."

"I thought we were safe now!" Tears began flowing down Alegria's face. Curt enveloped her in his arms as she began to cry harder.

Daniel turned to Martha, giving Curt space as he tried to soothe Alegria.

"When they stopped the car, did you yell out loud for them to stop? It felt like it was in my head," said Martha.

"You heard that?" He looked surprised. "I directed that at Curt. No one else has ever heard me talk to someone else, not at any distance. Curt can't hear me when I talk to my sister. And she can't hear me when I talk to Curt, either."

"What about me?" asked Curt as he returned to them.

"She heard me yell for you to stop the car," said Daniel.

"She heard you yell to me in my head? I didn't know anyone else could hear you talk to me. That's a new one," said Curt.

"Yes, it is," said Daniel.

Daniel glanced at Martha, and started to say something, but was cut off as Alegria stepped forward to join them.

"Can we go home? Now?" Alegria pleaded, her eyes still glistening with tears.

"Yes," said Daniel. "Martha, I'll call you if we find anything."

Chapter 13

S he watched as Curt, Alegria, and Daniel climbed into Daniel's silver pickup truck after Daniel checked under it for leaks. However, they didn't leave. Daniel was waiting for Martha to get into her car before he left. She hurried to her new car, checked the back seat, paused to check under it for any suspicious leaks, then got in and started the car. All seemed well. Martha drove out of the parking lot, and Daniel followed her for two blocks. Then, she turned north to Carrollton, while he turned south to take Alegria and Curt home to Dallas.

Parking in her usual parking spot outside her building induced a knot to form in Martha's stomach. She hadn't been home since the man with the gun had broken in. She walked slowly up the sidewalk, wary of shadows, to her door. The police line was gone. Entering the dark apartment, Martha's hands trembled. She clutched her keys in her hand as if it were a knife, ready to stab out at an attacker.

No attackers appeared, even after Martha checked all the closets, large cabinets, laundry room, and shower. Her heart, which had been beating in her throat from the moment she had entered the front door, began to slow. The sliding-glass door to the patio had been replaced with a newer model that had a lock at the base as well as on the handle. A maintenance slip from the apartment complex lay on the kitchen counter, showing that work had been done earlier in the day.

The love seat, rocking chair, and dusty books were as she had left them. The portrait of Mom and Dad was still on the mantelpiece on the wall. The room was as she'd left it, but the uneasy feeling that something was wrong stayed with Martha. Finally, she decided nothing had changed but her. Unpacking her suitcase took only a few minutes. Martha decided to shower, but took down the opaque decorative shower curtain, leaving only the clear plastic liner in place. She wanted to be able to see if someone were to come into the room. A new clothing rod hung in the closet. The complex must have replaced it as well. The other was in police evidence. Clothes lay in a heap on the floor. The door frame to the bedroom had been replaced and painted where it had broken when the door had been kicked open. The odor of the paint still lingered in the air.

Martha picked up and hung the skirts and blouses from the jumbled pile on the closet floor. She wanted to call Daniel. She wanted to know if power-steering fluid had been found on the driveway. It made no sense. If Rios and his associates were in custody, who had done this? Veronica's soon-to-be ex-husband? Why would he do it? Could someone else be trying to scare Curt and Alegria? Could someone be trying to kill them for a reason that hadn't been considered yet?

The phone rang, startling Martha out of her thoughts.

"Hello?"

"Martha Rowan?" Detective Monroe's voice filled Martha's ear. Disappointment that it wasn't Daniel calling engulfed her like a smothering blanket.

"This is Detective Monroe. I've spoken to Curt Holliczek about the incident earlier tonight regarding his car. We'd like you to come in and give us a statement tomorrow. Could you come in around nine a.m.?"

She cleared her throat to get rid of the smothering sensation. "Yes, Detective, I can come."

"I'll see you tomorrow. Goodnight."

A million questions occurred to Martha as soon as she hung up. Were there any leads on who had hired Rios? Had they discovered how he had known Curt's schedule? Had the house been checked for listening devices? Had the police checked Veronica's husband?

The conversation she'd had with Heidi a few days earlier came back to her mind. Who would inherit Alegria's uncle's money and property? Had he left a will? Could Alegria be a target now because she had inherited?

Martha pulled out her phone and looked up Daniel's number. The clock on the screen read 11:04 p.m.

Would he mind if I call this late? Would he think I'm intruding for asking questions about Alegria's uncle's will?

Why are you sticking your nose where it doesn't belong? What makes you think you can call him up like it's nothing? It's not as if you've ever easily called anyone in your entire life. He'd been going to say something before Alegria interrupted. Maybe he thinks you can hear all his thoughts. Maybe he's worried you heard something you shouldn't have. Maybe the police are right, and he did this because he's jealous of Alegria and Curt.

STOP! That's ridiculous. He wouldn't have stopped them if he'd wanted them injured. Think positively. No negativity allowed.

I WILL call him tomorrow. After I've had some sleep. After I've thought this through.

Sleep evaded Martha. When at last she drifted off, her dreams were broken jumbles of car accidents, blood, and bullets, followed by crying babies, and Daniel kissing Alegria. She awoke in a cold sweat, almost yelling, with a vision of herself in her new car hurtling toward a head-on collision with Alegria branded into her brain. Her breath was shallow; her heart was pumping right out of her rib cage through her sternum.

After dragging herself, exhausted, to work, Martha couldn't bear to tell Bill about what had happened to Alegria's car. He would worry. He'd think she was placing herself in danger by associating with them. Worse, he would probably be right. For her own safety, she should back off, but she didn't want to do it.

When she left the office an hour later to go see Detective Monroe, she took a cab, telling Bill only that the police needed her to go over a few details.

"Now, tell me what happened when you left the restaurant," began Detective Monroe after the two had sat down at his desk.

Martha paused. She didn't want to tell him that she'd noticed a leak, and that Daniel had seen it too because he had been reading her mind. The big detective was already annoyed with her for not taking his advice and avoiding the entire family.

"A second 'thank you' dinner?" he'd said, as if her actions had been perverse attempts to find more trouble. Instead, she said, "Right after they pulled away, Daniel and I both noticed the fluid on the ground where their car had been parked. Daniel called for them to stop, and they did. That's when they found the puncture in the power-steering fluid container."

He looked at her with disbelief in his eyes. Maybe his training told him that she was editing the story. He couldn't know what she was editing, only that something was being withheld. He didn't like it, the reticence she was displaying. The list of questions Martha had thought of the night before fled her brain in the face of his displeasure, leaving her tongue dry and uncoordinated. Words didn't flow as they should.

"Addison P.D. collected the video from the restaurant. They're sending it to me, but they say it's grainy and from a bad angle. But their synopsis does support your statement. Do you have anything else to add? Anything that might lend some insight into the family dynamics? Did the three Holliczeks get along well? Was there any tension between the brothers, or between Alegria and either of the men? Did they argue?"

"Between the Holliczeks? No, they got along well. They seemed happy that the whole thing was over. The only tension arose when we realized that someone had tampered with the car. Then, Alegria broke down in tears."

The detective's questions about the Holliczek family brought back both doubt and the forgotten questions. "Did you check on Veronica's husband?"

"I can't give you any details about that."

"Was a listening device found in the house? Did you check for one?"

"We did check, but again, I can't tell you what was or wasn't found. Can you tell me if you found Mrs. Holliczek to be unreasonable or emotionally volatile?"

"If she's been emotional, she's had good reasons. Her husband was almost killed. Her child almost kidnapped. Her uncle died. Then, yesterday her car was sabotaged. Given all that, I'd say she was doing as well as could be expected. I've seen her cry, but she never lashed out at anyone, and she wasn't unreasonable."

Leaving the police station, Martha realized Detective Monroe hadn't asked her any questions about Daniel. Either he didn't suspect him or he felt she couldn't be impartial in answering since Daniel had saved her life. She sat at her desk, lost in thought, her computer screen dark.

Another knot formed in her stomach as she contemplated the detective's suspicion of Alegria. Alegria had known that the baby was going to Curt's office that day. Maybe she had hired the kidnapper and known where he would take the baby. Maybe Curt hadn't been supposed to survive. Perhaps she was seeing someone else. Not Daniel, of course, but another man. Or, maybe she was mentally unstable. Would she risk sabotaging her own car? She could have been killed in an accident along with Curt. Was she suicidal? No, she'd had post-partum depression. That didn't mean she was suicidal. Not everyone who was depressed was suicidal. Besides, Daniel had said her treatment had worked well enough to save her marriage. Alegria didn't exhibit anything that looked like depression to Martha. On the other hand, maybe she needed money and knew she could extort it from her uncle if the baby were threatened. Although, if she was so close to her uncle, wouldn't she have simply asked him for the money?

What about Veronica? Veronica had volunteered to babysit Felix the day Curt had been shot. If she'd wanted the baby kidnapped, she wouldn't have done that. If she had needed money, wouldn't she, like Alegria, have simply asked her uncle for it? Besides, she seemed to enjoy taking care of Felix. She had fed him, bathed him, and taken care of him while he had been sick, when Alegria couldn't be there. Of course, Veronica may have had some other motive, but Martha didn't know her or the family well enough to know if past hurts or scarred childhoods might be involved.

Maybe it was Veronica's soon-to-be-ex-husband, Roberto. He was angry with her about the divorce. He had been at the house the day the car had been damaged. He could have planned the attack on Curt from Peru. His arrival in the United States after the attack might have been planned so he could oversee the payment of the ransom. Curt said Roberto was upset by Alegria's uncle's death, which might be true. Death was never part of the plan. With her uncle dead, Roberto couldn't extort money from him. Martha wanted Roberto to be guilty, mostly because she didn't know him, but she had to consider all the options.

Daniel. Could it have been Daniel? Why? Would he plot to kidnap his own nephew? Did he need money? Would he have known to hire a Peruvian mercenary for the job based on a few trips to Peru? He'd saved her life. Of course, killing her had been Rios' plan, to remove a witness. He hadn't been hired to attack her. Perhaps no one had been supposed to get hurt, and Daniel had been trying to stop a plot that had snowballed out of control when he had saved her. Would he do that? Could he be behind it all? Would he have stopped Alegria and Curt from driving away last night if he had wanted them dead? Or was it that he had to react when he realized that Martha had seen the puddle under the car, to take suspicion off himself?

A feeling of vertigo, of the world tipping over, hijacked Martha's mind. The police had told her to stay away from the Holliczeks, but she hadn't listened. If she was honest with herself, she would admit that she was attracted to Daniel. But could that handsome face, that charm, those eyes, and that unusual ability lead him to believe that the rules didn't apply to him? That laws were for other people? That even his own family didn't deserve respect and humane treatment? Martha didn't want to believe it.

She didn't want to believe Alegria might be crazy enough to kill, either. As for Veronica, she had no known motive. Roberto could be the guilty party, but Martha knew she couldn't decide that he was guilty just because she wanted him to be. Someone had to be guilty. Martha wished she could believe it was some faceless cartel member in Peru. The only one Martha felt safe ruling out was Curt. He'd come too close to death to be behind it all.

Stay away from them. For your own safety. A nameless cartel member didn't sabotage the power steering. How much do you really know about them? Nothing. So stay away.

The sound of ringing from her purse startled Martha out of her own head. She pawed through the bottom of her purse looking for her phone. The screen showed that Daniel

Holliczek was calling. Martha pressed ignore and dropped the phone back into her purse.

Forcing herself to focus on work, Martha finished only one task for the day, logged out, and went home. She didn't stop by Bill's office to tell him anything. He and Heidi had done enough. They didn't need the extra worry.

After completing her shoulder exercises and working her legs in the apartment complex recreation room, Martha turned her cell phone off. It had rung four times while she had exercised, and its ring tone was getting annoying. She didn't know how many more times she could resist answering it. According to the screen, she had now missed four calls from Daniel and one from Alegria. He'd left a message, but Martha didn't want to listen to it. She walked back to her apartment, taking care to pay attention to people around her and to approach blind corners with caution.

When she walked into the kitchen to get a glass of water, she saw that, on the counter, the message light on her answering machine was blinking. Inclined to ignore the flashing, Martha turned to leave the kitchen, but turned resolutely back and pushed the button. Her parents might have called. Hoping to hear one of her parents, but expecting to hear Daniel's voice, Martha braced herself against whatever he might say. She was startled to hear Heidi's voice floating on the air in slightly muffled, hollow recorded tones.

"Hello, Martha. It's Heidi. I hope you're doing well. Dr. Pierce's office called and left me a message asking that you call them. I think they have a question about your insurance. Call me and let me know how you are healing. If you need to chat about anything, I'm here. Bye."

Tears welled up and spilled down her face. Heidi and Bill were both so sweet to her. How had she managed to involve them in this mess? She couldn't dump any more trouble on them. It wouldn't be fair.

Another message clicked on and Alegria's voice came out, louder and more distressed than Heidi's. "Hi Martha, it's Alegria. I wanted to let you know that we did find more fluid from the car in our driveway. Daniel cleared out the garage for us last night, which was a project. He didn't finish until one a.m. We will be parking in the garage now. I had to practically sit on Curt to keep him from helping clean. I hope that you have had no more problems. Call and let me know how you are. Bye."

The machine clicked off. The tears were flowing freely, and Martha's sinuses closed. Breathing through her nose became impossible. She gulped air into a heaving chest and tried to calm down. Breathing required extra effort. Alegria, baby Felix, and Curt were still in danger. Fear filled the air and pressed in on Martha. Visions of them dead in a wreck flowed through her mind, followed by a vision of the lifeless, innocent baby in a small white coffin. Alegria with blood flowing down her face. Curt lying on the ground, shot, in a pool of blood. Martha felt as though she were choking and began to tremble all over. She'd been sweating from her exercises, but now the sweat poured out of her.

She rushed into the bathroom and ran the shower as cool as she could stand it. She stood under the water until she began to shiver. Her head was pounding. Martha fell into bed and covered her face with her damp towel.

Yelling out loud, Martha awoke from a nightmare, with a vision of the masked gunman jumping out from behind her front door replaying in her head. Her stomach growled. The clock said 8:04 p.m., and Martha realized she'd forgotten to eat dinner or even get water to drink after her workout. Her head still vaguely ached, probably from dehydration and hunger.

The wet towel had fallen off her face, making a cool, damp spot on her pillow. Martha swept it off the bed and tossed it on the floor in the bathroom as she passed by on her way to the kitchen. Hanging it up required too much effort.

She got a drink of water with as much ice as the cup would hold. The water didn't last long. Martha sat at her second-hand, wood-laminate-covered kitchen table crunching on the ice and decided she didn't have the energy to cook anything. She clicked on her laptop and read the news headlines. Nothing but earthquakes, war zone deaths caused by supposedly friendly forces, suppression of the press and freedom of speech in Russia, even worse suppression of rights in China, genocidal warfare in Africa, refugees, and the dangers of a warming planet.

Maybe local news would be better. Nope. Another man freed after losing fifteen years from being wrongly convicted of a crime. At least Dallas County had kept the evidence, so the wrongly convicted had some recourse. Lots of other states and counties hadn't bothered. How many wrongly convicted people languished behind bars? How many more had been executed? Not happy thoughts. Martha checked her social networking site on which she'd only connected to relatives and Lorena's family. Lorena had posted more pictures of Rome. Aunt Jeannie had a good cucumber crop. At last, something positive. A prayer request for Great-Aunt Harriet. That wasn't good. Pictures of a random cousin's puppy. Cute.

Music maybe. She opened a radio site. Music started. Matchbox Twenty's "Unwell." The song appealed to her.

The entire refrain hit home. Martha felt completely off. Her old self was gone, and in its place was this temporarily impaired person who could barely function. At least she wasn't as bad as the guy in the song. She wasn't talking to herself in public. Only in private. Not out loud. Only in her head. She should get more sleep, too.

Martha pulled an old *Calvin and Hobbes* collection book off the dusty shelf and went through the whole thing. The distraction took her mind off the Holliczek problem for a whole hour and a half. The moment she closed the book, that song began echoing through her brain. Stuck on repeat. Lying in bed, the song's refrain continued in Martha's head for the next hour. She tried all her usual tricks to stop it, but nothing worked tonight. Nothing remained to look forward to doing.

Daniel's amber eyes kept floating across her field of vision. Martha dreaded talking to him. She didn't want to tell him that she felt unsafe near his family. Someone had to be guilty, and she didn't know any of them well enough to judge who that might or might not be. Her heart seized up at the thought of seeing Daniel. He'd know what she was thinking. He would sense her fear of him, and he would be angry. That spark of fire she'd seen after dinner at Alegria's house would return.

The shadows were marching across the ceiling into the early hours of the morning before a troubled sleep replaced them with even worse nightmares. Consciousness returned abruptly in the predawn hours, with trembling limbs and memories of blood. Getting through the day at work wasn't going to be easy.

Make an appointment to see the doctor. You need therapy or counseling or treatment or something. You were supposed to follow up with the doctor. What about that prescription? Maybe you should fill it?

What, and then have to deal with medication side effects on top of everything else? No way!

What did that doctor prescribe, anyway? Anti-anxiety pills? An antidepressant? Antidepressants can increase suicidal thoughts in some people. You're not suicidal now, but maybe you will be if you take that medication. On the other hand, they wouldn't have prescribed it if it didn't help people. At least look at the prescription. Think about it. Google the name of the medication.

Martha fell asleep on the train on the way downtown. She was thankful when a fellow commuter who rode with her on an almost daily basis tapped her on the shoulder. Martha thanked the friendly faced, middle-aged woman profusely.

"Think nothing of it. I hope someone would wake me if I fell asleep. You look worn out. You must be working too hard. If you don't take care of yourself, you'll get sick." The woman gave a motherly, sympathetic smile and walked away.

Chapter 14

The day progressed in fits and starts as people wandered in and out of Martha's space. She conversed with Bill about files and work, but felt as though she were watching herself and everyone else from some point outside her body. She didn't have the emotional energy, nor the motivation, to care about anything. Everything required too much effort, effort she didn't have the strength or energy to produce.

Late in the day, Bill planted himself next to Martha's desk. "Did you make that follow-up appointment that the doctor at the hospital recommended?" he asked her, his arms crossed on his chest. Evading the question wasn't an option. The frown lines at the corners of his mouth were deep, and the eyes worried.

"No."

"Did you fill the prescription?"

"No."

"If you want, I'll ask Heidi to schedule the appointment for you. I can't stand here and watch you disintegrate before my eyes. You're moving like a ghost of yourself, and you aren't getting much done based on the reports I'm seeing. Did something else happen? I thought the police caught all the men involved?"

"Remember you told me to stay away from the Holliczek family? I should have listened."

"What happened?"

"I went to dinner to meet Curt, since he was finally released from the hospital. He was full of good humor and warmth.

Alegria and Daniel were wonderful. Dinner was lovely. Then we left the restaurant and found someone had sabotaged Alegria's car."

"Sabotaged how?"

"They punctured the power-steering fluid. She could have lost control of the vehicle. She and Curt could have died after dinner that night if Daniel and I hadn't seen the leaking fluid."

"So it's not over. At least not for them."

"I don't know who to trust. Detective Monroe seems to suspect Alegria and Daniel. Alegria's sister, Veronica, and her soon-to-be ex-husband are possible suspects, too. I'm afraid if I go near them, I'll be putting myself in danger. I've been avoiding their phone calls, but it feels cowardly, like a betrayal of their friendship. They've been so sweet to me, and I like them." Tears were welling up in Martha's eyes.

Bill reached over and patted Martha on her shoulder. "It will be all right. You need to take care of yourself before you deal with them. Come on with me. Let's get you a drink. You're coming back to my place. The PTSD is making everything look worse than it is." He took her hand and pulled her out of her seat, steering her toward the break room, where he bought her a bottle of tea from the vending machine.

"PTSD is not something you should mess around with. I've read several articles about soldiers coming home from Iraq and Afghanistan with it. Ignoring it makes things worse," said Bill.

Sniffling, Martha nodded her agreement and drank the tea. "I will make the doctor appointment. You and Heidi have done enough. I can handle it."

"Are you sure?"

"Yes." She moved her lips into a near smile, though her face was still red and blotchy.

On the train ride home, Martha examined all the other passengers to make sure they all looked familiar. Two didn't, but neither looked to be interested in her, which was a relief. She looked over her shoulder, under her car, and inside her car when she arrived at the Park and Ride. The rearview mirror and side-view mirrors got more use on the way to her apartment than they'd ever had in any single car trip. Once, Martha was so busy watching behind and next to her that she had to slam on the brakes to avoid hitting a car in front of her that had slowed to turn right.

By the time Martha arrived home, her hands were cramped from gripping the steering wheel too tightly. Sweat trickled down Martha's neck the instant she left her air-conditioned car. The late afternoon heat had reached its peak of about one hundred degrees. Martha trudged up the sidewalk, around the side of the house-like, gabled buildings, and between the holly bushes to her door. Thinking entirely about getting out of the heat, Martha was no longer paying any attention to her surroundings.

As she inserted her key in her door, a voice behind her said, "Martha."

"Ahhhh!" Martha screamed and jumped.

Daniel was standing behind her.

"I'm sorry! I didn't mean to surprise you." He put both hands up in front of him as if to stop her from attacking him. He wore black slacks, an aqua-blue polo shirt, and black leather shoes, as if he had come straight from work.

"You scared me! Why are you here?"

"I've been trying to reach you for the last two days, but you haven't answered. I was afraid something had happened to you."

"Oh. No, nothing. I'm fine."

"You don't look fine. You look upset. What happened? Can I help?"

The tears welled up again and began to stream down Martha's face. Turning away from him, she buried her face in her hands, leaned into her front door, and began sobbing.

Daniel came up behind her and put a hand on one of her heaving shoulders. "It's okay. Whatever it is. If you can't say it, think it. I'll get it. If you don't want me to know, think the word 'no,' and I'll leave."

Martha let memories of the doctor telling her she had PTSD, the feelings of suffocation and doom, the nightmares, and the sleepless nights flow through her mind. She envisioned her fear driving home. The song from the radio played in the background, stuck on the refrain.

"I'm so, so sorry. I didn't know." Daniel turned her away from the door and pulled her to him, his chin resting on the top of her head. He closed her in his arms and stroked her hair until she stopped crying. Then he took the key from her hand, unlocked the door, and walked her inside.

"It makes perfect sense, you know," he said as he searched her white kitchen cabinets for glasses, filled one with ice and water, and handed it to her. "You've been shot at twice, and you were standing near Curt when he got shot. You had to save his life with him bleeding all over the place. You were forced into a car accident in which your vehicle rolled and your shoulder was separated. You've had weeks of hell almost as bad as any soldier might see in a battle zone. I've seen a lot of good people get PTSD. You can't ignore it. You have to deal with it."

"That's what Bill said."

"Good for Bill. I know you saw a doctor. Did you get any prescriptions? Have you followed up?"

"I got a prescription. It's in a drawer upstairs. I didn't fill it because I was afraid it would have bad side effects or would make me worse. You know all those commercials on television say 'Talk to your doctor about blah-blah-blah drug,' and then they end with a horrifying list of possible side effects. The doctor says you can't just stop taking those things. You have to taper off them. What if it didn't work or I reacted badly to it and I couldn't just stop taking it? It didn't seem worth the risks. I thought I could handle the stress myself without the medication."

"If you don't want to take medication, you could try therapy only, but I don't know how that works. A guy I know took the medicine and was glad he did."

"You know someone who took medicine for PTSD?"

"Of course. I'm in the Army. The Army's gotten pretty good about convincing people that this needs to be treated."

"I thought they still had a high suicide rate?"

"They do. That's because they haven't managed to treat depression like they treat post-traumatic stress. You'd think it would fall in the same category, but for some reason it doesn't."

"So you think I should fill the prescription?"

"I would, but it's entirely up to you. If you want to talk to another doctor about it first and find out your options, that's fine. Just don't wait to see a doctor."

Daniel picked the phone up off the counter. "Here, call your doctor now. This thing can eat away at your ability to accomplish anything, including making a simple phone call. If I leave and you haven't called, you may decide it takes too much effort. This is an insidious condition, like depression. Your own mind is working against you and telling you that nothing can be done and nothing will help. You've got to fight your own brain."

"I've been doing that most of my life anyway. Lately, it seems like I don't have the strength to fight." Martha stared at the phone he'd handed her, pulled out her cell phone, looked up the number in her contact list, and dialed it on her home phone.

Daniel stood and watched as she made the appointment. When she disconnected the call, he took the phone and set it back on the counter for her. "Good job. That's the first step. If you want, I can take you to fill the prescription."

"I don't know if I can take another sleepless night. The medicine would probably help me sleep, too, wouldn't it? Could we go to the pharmacy? I don't think I have the energy to drive myself."

"Absolutely! Let's go."

After thirty minutes of wandering the aisles of the corner drug store while waiting for the prescription, Daniel and Martha got back in his gray truck to go.

"I caught you coming home from work. Did you want to get some dinner?" said Daniel.

"I don't think I want to go to a restaurant. I'll have a bowl of cereal at home."

You've caused him enough trouble.

"It's no trouble."

"You must have been a pain to live with as a child. How did anyone put up with you?" Martha teased. "Can you turn that off, or do you always hear what people don't want to say?"

"It doesn't turn off. I've gotten used to the fact that everyone dissembles, to some extent. I won't say people always lie. However, they have their own motivations and purposes that may cause them to leave out information, or not fully explain why they do or don't do things. What's weird for me is that you can hear my answers to your thoughts. Can you hear my thinking, too?"

"No, all I hear are responses. Which, by the way, seems unfair. You get all the information on me and how I think, but I can't know why you do what you do or what your motivations are."

"Is that your way of asking me if I'm plotting to kill my brother and sister-in-law for some nefarious purpose of my own?" Though his tone was teasing, the expression of his face was serious, unsmiling.

I don't know you.

He answered her verbally this time. "Yes, you do. I didn't do anything to harm Curt or Alegria. I would never endanger them, or Felix."

"I *want* to believe you," said Martha. She didn't feel comfortable conversing in her head. It felt surreal.

"I know."

"I need time. I'd like to trust you." In her brain, she wondered what emotions he could sense, but she stifled the thought.

Daniel either hadn't caught the thought or was polite enough to pretend he hadn't caught it. "That's a start at least. How about dinner? If you don't want to go out, we could order something. A pizza? Chinese? Pick up from a restaurant of your choice?"

"A pizza sounds good."

"Toppings? I'm a sausage and bell pepper guy, but if you prefer something else, speak up."

"I like pepperoni, bell pepper, and mushrooms."

"Okay, let's order one."

They arrived at Martha's apartment a moment later and went inside. After considering the merits of Pizza House over Uncle Joe's, Daniel called to place the order.

Martha went to the kitchen to get drinks, thinking about whether to try to guard her thoughts or be as honest as possible. She could see all kinds of complications. He came into the kitchen to find her.

"The pizza will be here in twenty to thirty minutes."

"You must have a terrible time dating." The words were out of Martha's mouth before she could stop them.

Daniel laughed. "I do okay."

"I mean, you must know when whoever you're out with bends to suit you. If I'd agreed to sausage and bell pepper, but while we ate, I sat and thought how I'd have preferred pepperoni, you'd know. If you went out with someone who did that, you'd know your date wasn't happy, but that it was her own fault for not speaking up. I imagine it could interfere with all sorts of other things besides food."

A huge grin crossed his face. "People do compromise a lot. I find I get along best with the ones who compromise in a way that's a real compromise and not a surrender. If both parties are happy, things are definitely better."

Martha's face lit on fire as it occurred to her what other things he might be thinking a date might not be open about. She was glad she was standing across the kitchen from him.

"Do all your friends and family know you can hear them thinking?"

"No. In fact, very few people outside my immediate family know."

"Then why did you tell me?"

"I didn't." He sat in a mismatched chair at her table and watched her put ice into glasses.

"Yes, you did. You answered my thoughts at the restaurant. I heard you respond in my head." She was glad he had chosen to stay so far away. She realized suddenly that he'd done it to give her privacy in her thoughts. Putting distance between himself and others probably allowed him to get along better with people. He was saved from the distraction of hearing thoughts and prevented from knowing things he shouldn't know or didn't want to know. If he'd been hearing other people's thoughts all his life, he might automatically put space between himself and others, a self-protection mechanism for dealing with receiving too much information in his head.

"I've answered people's thoughts in my head thousands of times in my life. No one has ever heard me and responded other than my siblings. It's never happened before. You shocked me when you called me on being in your head. No one ever caught me like that before. It was almost as disconcerting for me as it was for you." He stood up and moved toward her to take the glass she held out for him.

The idea of Daniel coming near her and hearing her thoughts, and of being able to hear him answer, was mind-numbing. Martha blurted out, "It's a good thing you don't tell people." Even the roots of her hair went red as she realized how silly that sounded and tried again. "I mean, know-ing you can hear me makes me want to keep my distance and think smarter, more witty thoughts. It makes me nervous. I'll bet your siblings were all honest as kids. You'd know if they were lying. Or did you extort money from them, or have them do your chores, in exchange for your silence?"

Daniel returned to the other side of the kitchen and sat, relaxed in every line of his body, at the table again. His feet were kicked out and crossed at the ankle. His drink was grasped loosely in his fingertips, which were resting on the table. "I guess honesty prevailed. My parents knew what I could do. They recognized when they needed to talk to a child who was avoiding sitting by me or standing near me. Avoidance was a sign something was troubling them. I didn't extort either favors or money. We didn't have any money, and my parents would have noticed if someone else was doing my chores."

What Martha most wanted to know, she refused to ask. Why she could hear him, Martha didn't know and doubted he knew either. She was afraid to consider it significant, especially if he was perplexed about it rather than excited by it. Time to change the subject.

They discussed what university each had attended, what they had studied, and student life experiences until the pizza arrived.

Not sitting at the table to eat with Daniel would be rude, so Martha set the table for two and joined him at the table. She felt completely awkward, not knowing what to say, half afraid of any thoughts that might flow through her head.

Daniel's charming grin appeared. His amber eyes lit. "Thanks for daring to sit near me. I know it's hard, but you'll get so used to it, you'll forget eventually. Be yourself. I've heard people think all sorts of things, and it's made me analyze my own thoughts. I'm no better in my mind than anyone else: silly, conceited, self-absorbed, fragmented, and uninteresting. If it makes you feel any better, what I hear from you is mostly concern for others. You don't want to be a nuisance, or cause anyone trouble. And you're a lot less interested in your own external appearance than most of women I've met. What I see in you does you credit. If anything, the only flaw I've seen is that you don't like to accept help. I know you have a hard time talking to people, but you do it anyway. You're brave." He paused and smiled, and her heart fluttered.

"I'm not brave; everything makes me anxious," she said.

"So, you're anxious. You show up anyway. Besides, you're already pretty good at controlling your anxiety. You know how to beat back your demons. I heard you at the hospital."

"I don't always win. In college, my friend Lorena had to help me get past my anxiety and through some doors."

"When you follow up with your doctor, a psychologist will be able to teach you techniques to control anxiety. The medicine will help, too. I know how it feels to be uncomfortable in a crowd. Maybe your senses take in too much for you, too," he said.

She laughed. "Not like yours do!"

"You're sure you don't hear me, right?" he asked.

"No, not unless you answer me. I think you have to talk directly to me. That's what you do with Curt, right? He can't hear your thoughts, can he?"

"No. I guess it's like with my siblings then."

Great! Exactly how I wanted to be categorized—like a sister.

"Believe me, I know you aren't at all like my sister."

"Daniel! Don't do that!"

"Sorry, I'll try not to. Sometimes, I answer automatically. I'm not used to you hearing me."

"Then do it verbally."

"Okay, okay." His eyes twinkled, laughter dancing in the amber.

Martha knew he would do it again, but she didn't mind. She'd adapt, like his siblings had adapted. It wasn't as if he could turn it off.

They started eating the warm, cheesy pizza.

Daniel's phone began to ring.

He glanced at it. "It's Curt. Sorry, but I'd better see what he wants."

"Hello?" After a moment, he continued. "Which hospital? Uh-huh. What can I do? Okay. I'll be there shortly."

Chapter 15

Martha stopped mid-bite when the word "hospital" came out of Daniel's mouth. He clicked off his phone and answered the question she was waiting to ask.

"Alegria had an allergic reaction to something she ate. She has a shellfish allergy. She went to dinner with Veronica and Roberto to play peacekeeper while they reviewed business documents. The waiter served her something with shellfish accidentally."

"Are they sure it was an accident?"

Daniel's face went stony and his eyes focused inward as he considered the question. "I don't know. From what Curt said, I don't think anyone has considered that it might not be an accident. Why would someone do that? It makes no sense. No, the server made an error, delivered the wrong dish to the wrong table. That must be it."

Martha thought he was trying hard to convince himself that it had to be an accident. She saw him register the thought, but he didn't comment.

"I'm suspicious of everything right now. I see attacks everywhere. I'm anxious about everything. Do you need to go?" she asked.

"Yes, Veronica and Roberto need to finish the paperwork, and Curt wants to stay with Alegria, so I'm going to babysit Felix."

"What a good uncle you are. Can you finish your pizza first or do you have to go right now?"

"If you don't mind I'll eat quickly, and then run."

He was done with a second piece and his drink before Martha had finished her first. She wiped her hands quickly and walked him to the door.

"Thanks for coming over. I guess I needed someone to check on me."

"Keep your doctor's appointment, and I'll know I've helped. I'll call soon." He walked away.

"Let me know how Alegria is!" Martha called to his back. He swung around and waved in reply.

The pizza was getting cold by the time Martha finished her second piece. Then she began to clean up the kitchen.

You should have offered to let him take some with him. He left in such a hurry. No hug, no kiss on the cheek. Maybe he's pulling back. He was only checking on you because he feels guilty that you got dragged into this.

Stop!

Martha shook her head. She could feel the anxiety knotting up her stomach again. The thoughts were only going to get worse if she didn't try to redirect them. The pills. She hadn't taken the prescription yet. If she was going to sleep tonight without worrying about Alegria being poisoned or whether she had said stupid things to Daniel, she should look at those pills.

With the plates shoved hastily into the sink, Martha dried her hands and pulled the white paper bag emblazoned with the pharmacy name out of her purse. Attached to the bag were two pages of directions, warnings of drug interactions and possible side effects. A quick glance confirmed her worst fears about the side effects. The commercials on television weren't kidding. Taking the medication could make her feel better, but it could also cause an allergic reaction with breathing difficulties, or make her suicidal. Great.

She stared at the pill in her hand. The small white oval seemed simultaneously insignificant and stunningly danger-ous. The risk of taking the pills seemed too great to justify any possible benefit. Yet, the doctor had prescribed it, so it must have gone through testing. How many medications had been in the news, pulled off the market as unforeseen, and deadly side effects appeared after the testing phase was well over?

If Daniel hadn't told her that he would take it, and that he knew people who had benefitted from it, she would have dumped it back into the plastic bottle and tossed it into the back of her cabinet, never to be seen again.

Martha broke the pill in half and dropped one half back in the bottle, per the instructions. She popped the other half into her mouth, washed it down with water, and decided not to think about the side effects. She watched an evening tele-vision detective show, wasted an hour on her computer, and went to bed.

AT SIX-THIRTY THE next morning, the alarm went off. Martha awoke, surprised to realize how deeply and peacefully she had slept.

Getting to work was smoother than expected. On the way to the Park and Ride, her knuckles no longer whitened on the steering wheel every time a car honked. The people on the train all looked like the same commuters who were there every day. No one seemed suspicious. The middle-aged, motherly woman who had awakened Martha the time she had fallen asleep now smiled and nodded hello. Martha relaxed and read all the way downtown.

By lunch time, Martha found herself smiling and humming to herself at her desk. The hole she'd dug herself into at work wasn't as big as she'd thought. With some effort, she could catch up to where she wanted to be within a couple of days or maybe a week. After dividing out similar tasks, grouping related file work, and prioritizing items, nothing seemed impossible.

When Bill came by, Martha gave him a confident smile and handed him the report he was most likely seeking.

He studied her face for a second before smiling back at her. "You look well today. Are you feeling better?"

"Much better. I filled the prescription the doctor gave me. I wish I had done it sooner, but I was afraid the side effects would be awful."

"I am so glad to hear that. You followed up with the doctor, too?"

"I have an appointment for lunch time tomorrow. I'll take a long lunch and stay late."

"Perfect. Thanks for the report." Bill waved and walked back to his office.

That evening, Martha stood on her patio wearing gardening gloves and surveyed her potted plants. She kept forgetting about their existence. A few well-timed thunderstorms had helped most of them survive, but two in smaller pots had perished due to neglect. She pulled the leafless, lifeless stems from the pots and dumped the leftover dirt onto the grass outside the patio. A couple of the larger Aloe vera plants needed dividing, but that could wait. After deadheading the potted miniature rose and collecting the detritus, Martha stepped back into her apartment and firmly latched the sliding-glass door.

The ringing of the phone caught her attention as she washed her hands. She quickly dried them and went to the phone. "Hello?"

"Hi, Martha, it's Alegria. How are you?"

"I'm great!" Martha said, realizing that she meant it. "How are you? Daniel told me about your allergic reaction."

"I'm much better. I always swell up when I have shrimp, so I avoid it. The waiter made a mistake at the restaurant. I got someone else's shrimp enchiladas instead of the chicken enchiladas I ordered. The mix-up wasn't apparent until I bit into it. By then, all I could do was use my EpiPen and go to the emergency room. Anyway, I was calling to invite you to coffee and shopping with me Saturday morning. Are you free?"

Saturday morning coffee and shopping with Alegria sounded great. Martha fleetingly thought of her plan to stay away from the family, but that idea had been blasted when Daniel had come to check on her and ended up staying for dinner. Not to mention that today it felt as if she had overreacted. "Yes, I'd love to go."

"Why don't you meet me at ten a.m in the chocolate shop in the Galleria? They have wonderful mocha drinks."

"Yes. Okay. That sounds great." Martha hadn't been shopping in the Galleria yet. She assumed that a lot of it might be out of her price range, but she could just window shop.

After ending the call, Martha stared at her phone and remembered that Daniel had said he would call. He hadn't. Had he forgotten? Or was he too busy?

The phone began to buzz in her hand, and Daniel's name appeared on the screen.

"Hello?"

"Hi, it's Daniel."

"Are you sure you can only hear thoughts from a few feet away?"

"Um, yes. Why?"

"Because I was just thinking that you hadn't called me."

His deep laugh came across the line. "Oh. No, I didn't know you were thinking that, I promise. Alegria's fine, by the way. I don't think the allergic reaction was an attack on her. Most likely, the wait staff at the restaurant made a mistake."

"I spoke to Alegria right before you called. We're going to get coffee and go shopping Saturday morning."

"Ah, her favorite activities. She took quite a liking to you. I hope you don't mind, but I expect she's going to be attempting her other favorite activity."

"What's that?"

"Matchmaking. She's been trying to set me up with friends of hers since shortly after she and Curt got married. She's angling for a sister-in-law that she likes." He sounded slightly exasperated.

"You don't appreciate the help?" Martha grinned, teasing him.

"No, I prefer to ask people out myself, and not have her do it for me. Which brings me to why I called. If you can stand to be around another Holliczek Saturday, after you're done with Alegria, would you like to go out with me?"

Martha realized the confident note had left his voice. He sounded like he feared she might turn him down. "I'd love to go out with you. What did you have in mind?"

"A picnic dinner at Shakespeare in the Park in Addison Circle. The play is *Much Ado About Nothing.*"

"That's wonderful. I've never been to Shakespeare in the Park, but I saw the ads for it. It sounds fun. What do I bring?"

"Well, I'll provide the picnic, water, a bottle of wine, and a blanket to sit. Why don't you bring the mosquito repellant?"

"I'm glad you mentioned that. I'd have forgotten it."

"We'll be there at dusk. Prime mosquito- chomping time, but it's worth it. I'll pick you up at six, okay?"

"Okay, see you then." She smiled as she disconnected the phone.

The mosquitos in Dallas during a wet summer appeared in enormous numbers from dusk to early morning. During the daytime, the bloodthirsty bugs haunted the shaded areas under trees, especially near water. In spite of public service announcements asking people to dump out any standing water, which provided the perfect habitat for the larvae to grow and mature, the mosquitos proliferated. Mosquito-borne illnesses such as West Nile exploded in the population during wet years. When that happened, the city resorted to aerial spraying to limit the numbers of the troublesome insects. Citizens of the Metroplex were advised not to go out without repellant.

A Shakespeare comedy with a picnic sounded like the perfect date. Martha remembered how her mom had worried that she'd never meet anyone in such a big city, being so shy. She'd urged Martha to try to get out of her shell, though "shell" was never the right word. "Concrete bunker" would have been more accurate. Mom would be pleased. Martha would have to call and tell her mom about it when she got back from her cruise next week.

Friday passed quietly. Dr. Pierce gave Martha a long list of names to call for therapy, after reassuring her about the medication the hospital doctor had prescribed.

Saturday morning, Martha sat at a bistro table in front of the chocolate shop in the Galleria mall. Her brown hair hung loosely around her shoulders over the pink blouse she had selected to wear with khaki capris and brown sandals. She'd been trying for a dressier look than her usual Saturday shorts and T-shirt. She didn't want to look out of place in the Galleria. Watching the variety of clothing on the people who strolled into view, she noticed she need not have worried about it.

Some people were very stylish, with expensive brand-name purses and shoes and well-cut clothes, but others would fit in at any mall anywhere. Glancing at her watch, she wondered if she had the right place, since it was five minutes after ten o'clock. Then, Alegria came into view, weaving around other shoppers, waving as she hurried toward Martha. Her hair was loose today, too. She walked with practiced ease on four-inch-high, strappy gold sandals. A simple but colorful sun dress revealed her smooth, brown shoulders and swung around her knees.

"I am sorry I am late. Felix didn't want me to leave without him this morning. I had to sneak out while Curt was distracting him. He is at a very clingy stage," she said in her clipped, accented English as she greeted Martha with a traditional hug and air kiss next to the cheek.

They sat together at the table, Martha drinking a luxuriously rich cocoa and cream milkshake while Alegria had a whipped-cream-covered, iced mocha drink. The questions Martha wanted to ask were rattling around in her head as she attempted to make small talk about Felix and the weather. Finally, she decided to simply ask what Alegria thought.

"Do you think Veronica's husband is behind the attack on you and Curt?"

"I never would have thought it of him. He has always been a very generous and considerate person. Goodness knows how patient he was with Veronica for the last six years. She is not an easy person to live with. We were raised very permissively. She has been used to getting her own way and does not compromise well. Curt would tell you I am the same, but he's never had to live with Veronica for more than a few weeks. Veronica has good business sense and can be very efficient in organizing things, but she does what is most logical to her without regard to the opinions or feelings of others. She steps on people's toes and feels they are in the wrong because they disagree with her. Veronica and Roberto have not had a comfortable marriage trying to run a business together. He believes in making clients for life through loyalty and generosity. She felt the clients would take advantage of them if they were not firm. They argued quite a lot. Most of the paperwork he wants her to complete is about dividing the business assets. She does not wish to face the fact that both the business *and* the marriage failed."

"What sort of business was it?"

"A woven goods export business. Many people weave beautiful textile materials in Peru: rugs, sweaters, hats, gloves, wall hangings. They even sold yarn and dyed wools."

"So you don't think he could be responsible for all the things that have happened?" Martha wanted to identify the source of the attacks. Pinning all the trouble on the unknown Roberto would have been simplest.

"He would have no motive. He is very well off financially and comes from a wealthy family himself. At least Roberto and Veronica do not have to argue over personal assets. Both signed prenuptial agreements that apply in case of divorce with no children. Both had a considerable amount of money going into the marriage. Veronica wasn't ready to have children. Roberto wanted children. It was another source of contention."

If Roberto was innocent, no known suspects were left. "Why would someone sabotage your car? If your uncle is dead, it can't be to extort money from him. Did you inherit his money?"

"No. That is to say, I inherited control of it, but not possession of it. Tío left his money in a trust for Felix until he is twenty-one years old. Curt and I administer the trust. Killing us would not get anyone the money. It would still go to Felix."

"What if they killed all of you, including Felix?"

"Well, Veronica would get half the trust, but the rest would be divided between about a hundred second and third cousins."

"How much would Veronica get?"

Alegria stared at Martha, a perplexed look in her eyes. "You can't think she would do this? She is my sister. Besides, she inherits Tio's properties, which will be worth quite a lot eventually."

"I don't want to think anyone would try to kill your family, but someone is trying. If not for the money, what other reason could there be?"

"None that I know of." Alegria sipped her drink, getting whipped cream on her upper lip before hastily wiping it away with a napkin.

"What about all those second and third cousins? Would they do it for the money?" Martha grasped at the last option she could see to solve the mess.

"I don't think they were informed that they were secondary beneficiaries. Since we are alive, there is no reason to tell them."

"Oh." The hope for a simple answer had evaporated. Of course, if it had been simple and obvious, the police would have found the answer by now. It wasn't as if they weren't investigating.

"Let's not think about this now," Alegria said firmly, shaking her head. "I have thought it over so much, it makes my head ache. Curt and I have gone over everything. The police are looking into our finances and have spoken to all of our friends, trying to discover if either of us are having affairs. We are not having affairs. We did see a counselor last year for a few months, which was very helpful. I learned about my post-partum depression and began treatment. Once we identified why I was falling apart and blaming him, we were both able to see what to do to fix things. If anything, our marriage is stronger for it. I can stop taking medicine soon. I have already started decreasing my dose. Our finances are okay. We don't need money. The police have even spoken to Daniel's commanding officer in the Reserves, and all his coworkers. They are looking in the wrong places." Alegria banged her hand emphatically on the bistro table, making it rock slightly.

Martha grabbed her drink to stabilize it.

"I'm sorry," said Alegria, grabbing a napkin to swipe up the few drops that had sloshed from the drinks. "I get so mad thinking that they are wasting time looking for evidence to make me or Daniel guilty. I can't think about this anymore. Let's go shopping. Are you ready?"

"Yes." Martha picked up her drink.

Both women walked down the wide halls of the mall, past the attached lobby of The Westin Hotel, looking at fancy dresses and household décor.

As they reached a small jewelry shop, Alegria began to laugh. "Whenever I see jewelry stores, I remember the time I went shopping with Veronica to find jewelry to wear to a fancy event in Peru. A friend had invited her to a government affair at an embassy. She had a ball gown to wear and needed jewelry to go with it. We went from shop to shop to shop, for two days. Finally, around three in the afternoon on the second day, Veronica found the perfect set of jewels: earrings, bracelet, and necklace in matched diamonds and sapphires. In Peru, you understand, prices are always negotiable. So Veronica and the owner haggled back and forth over the price of the jewels for five hours. The shop was supposed to have closed at six p.m., but she did not leave until eight o'clock. The store owner finally gave in and gave her the price she wanted, just to get her out of the store. Heaven knows, he never wished to see her in his store again. I almost fell asleep waiting on a bench outside the store. My feet were killing me from all the walking we had done, but Veronica didn't seem tired at all. She could have negotiated with that man until midnight! It's very rare that she doesn't get her own way. I think that is what most upsets her about this divorce. She did not want it, so she came here to avoid it, which only made Roberto follow her."

As they walked, Martha was relieved to find that Alegria had come mainly to window shop. Many stores carried items well beyond what Martha was willing to pay for any single item. The pair of white leather sandals Alegria had bought had been on summer clearance. They were beautiful and of a quality that would last. Martha would have bought a pair herself if they'd had her size available.

As noon approached, Martha began to get hungry and looked longingly at the restaurants they walked past. She was about to make her excuses and leave when Alegria took up the subject of lunch.

"You should come home to lunch with me. Daniel will be there doing some things around the house, so that Curt won't try to do them himself. I know he would like to see you." Her eyes sparkled and the hint she was giving was obvious.

"I'm already going to see him today. He asked me to go see Shakespeare in the Park with him tonight."

"He did? Good for him. You like him? He is quite handsome and has a good job. I know he can seem abrupt, but it is because he is two steps ahead of everyone by hearing their thoughts. Since he knows what to expect, he has already moved to the next subject. Though he does it on the phone, too, so perhaps it has become a habit. Regardless, he can be charming when he wants to be."

Martha said, "Um-hum." She knew exactly how bedazzling the combination of those oddly colored eyes with that lovely smile could be.

"Do come to my house. It isn't far from here. We can have a quick lunch, and then you can go get ready for your date. Please come." Alegria smiled, raised her eyebrows, and then squeezed Martha's arm lightly, while swinging the bag containing her sandals in the other hand.

"All right." Martha wasn't sure why she was agreeing, other than that Alegria clearly wanted her to come.

Chapter 16

Martha followed Alegria's car to her house, which was only about five minutes away. As they pulled onto her street, Martha saw Daniel's familiar pickup truck pull into the driveway. Curt and Daniel got out, and then Daniel reached into the back seat to release Felix from his car seat. Alegria honked her horn as she approached, and both men stopped walking up the drive upon seeing her. They waited for her to park. Curt approached Alegria's car as Daniel turned his attention to Martha's car.

"Hi," said Daniel. "I didn't expect to see you here." He wore old jeans and a T-shirt, both dotted with paint and grease stains and clearly used for yard work, and both of which emphasized his lean, athletic musculature.

"I know. Alegria insisted on inviting me to lunch." Her heart beat faster as Daniel smiled at her and closed her car door for her after she had gotten out.

They turned to walk to the front door with Curt and Alegria, who was holding her fussing son.

"Felix's hungry. We needed longer screws to fix the fence in the back yard, so we ran to the hardware store. I guess we took too long for him," said Daniel.

Curt, who was standing by the front door, violently pushed Alegria away from the house, and yelled "Get back!"

Curt dove away from the front door. Daniel grabbed Martha's arm and pulled her behind his back.

A ball of fire exploded from the house. The windows shattered outward. Pieces of glass and wood and brick flew up and rained down on Martha and Daniel. She covered her head with her hands, so she couldn't see Alegria, Curt, or Felix, but when the sound of the blast subsided she could hear Felix screaming over the roar of flames.

Daniel was up and running back toward the house. Curt lay on the lawn, debris strewn around him and on top of him. Chunks of brick lay near his head. Alegria was a few feet in front of him, curled around Felix, but moving. Burning scraps of wood frame, brick, and furniture littered the lawn around them. Daniel knelt next to Curt. He checked for a pulse before grabbing his brother by both arms and dragging him away from the burning house, toward the street.

Martha watched in horror as the flames burned higher, engulfing the roof. She got out her phone and dialed 911. Once the operator said she was dispatching a fire engine, Martha disobeyed the woman's request to stay on the line and hung up. Martha ran to assist Daniel as he directed a disoriented Alegria, carrying her wailing son, to sit on the grass next to her unconscious husband. As Daniel took the crying baby from Alegria and bounced him slowly in his arms, Martha remembered to call Detective Monroe.

The smell of natural gas drifted on the wind with the smoke as she dialed the number.

After a moment or two choosing the correct option to get a live person and then being transferred through the police department phone system, finally Martha heard the detective's voice on the line. "Detective Monroe, the Holliczek house exploded in front of me, and I smell gas," she said.

"Get away from the house. I'll be there soon. Is anyone injured?"

"Yes. Curt is unconscious and Alegria is dizzy. They have cuts all over them."

"Did you call 911?" he asked.

"Yes," she said.

A minute later, talking on the phone became impossible as the fire engine arrived, so Martha ended the call and sat beside Alegria. She put her arm around the crying woman. Daniel set Felix in Martha's lap, and turned his attention to Curt, who was starting to move.

Within five minutes of the explosion, firefighters turned water to the flames as paramedics examined Curt, Alegria, and Felix.

Martha refused their attention, although her ears were still ringing.

Events occurred in a blur. Sometime later, the ambulance carrying Curt, Alegria, and Felix left and Detective Monroe arrived at the scene.

The firefighters called in a second engine and evacuated the neighboring houses. They set up a perimeter halfway down the block and moved Daniel, Martha, and the police behind it.

Watching the house burn, Martha began to shake as she realized how close they had all come to dying.

"We're okay." Daniel's voice came clearly into her head. She looked at him. He was talking to Detective Monroe, running one hand through his dark, thick hair, his back to her.

Looking back at the house, Martha realized she didn't know where Veronica was. Had she been inside when it exploded?

"No. She left earlier with Roberto."

Detective Monroe and Daniel turned to Martha.

"We're going to the station to take statements. Will you come with me to the car?" the detective asked, looming over her in his oddly comforting way, his face lined with perpetual sadness.

"What about Alegria and Curt and Felix?"

"They're okay. Curt's probably got a concussion from the force of the blast, and he may have torn some stitches. Alegria's going to have a headache, too. Felix's okay. They took him in out of an abundance of caution, and because Alegria wouldn't leave without him. Curt was pretty well awake by the time the ambulance left. He was talking to me as they wheeled him away." Daniel put his hand out and brushed ashes from Martha's thick brown hair as he spoke.

Martha could see Detective Monroe watching as Daniel gently stroked her hair.

"Okay, let's get out of here." Martha turned and walked with the two men to a waiting car.

Martha sat and waited in a room by herself while Detective Monroe talked to Daniel. After about forty-five minutes, the big detective came in to see her. He smiled apologetically.

"Sorry to keep you waiting. I wanted to get a picture of what happened at the house this morning before I came to talk to you." He sat his bulk down on a chair and opened the file he had with him.

"I kept telling myself I should have listened to your advice and stayed away from the Holliczek family, but they are such good people, I couldn't do it. Something terrible is happening to their family, and they don't know why."

"Have you spoken to them about it?" he asked.

"Alegria and I met for coffee and shopping this morning, and we discussed what might be behind it all. She honestly doesn't know. No one seems to have a good motive that might explain all these attacks."

"What time did you meet Mrs. Holliczek?"

"She arrived at the mall at five minutes after ten this morning. We had drinks and then wandered the mall for a couple hours."

"How did you come to be with her at her house this afternoon?"

"Around noon she invited me back to her house for lunch. We got there just as Curt, Daniel, and the baby were arriving. They waited for us to park, and we all started toward the house together."

Detective Monroe nodded. "Go on."

"Daniel came over to talk to me. Curt and Alegria were ahead of us. The baby was fussy because he was hungry. Curt opened the door. He yelled, "Get back." Then, he dove away from the house. Somehow, he pushed Alegria and Felix ahead of him, away from the house. The whole place blew up."

Detective Monroe pushed the paperwork and a pen across the table toward her.

Martha sighed and started to fill out yet another formal statement.

An hour later, Martha handed her paperwork back to Detective Monroe and found Daniel waiting for her.

"I talked to Alegria on the phone. She and Felix are being released from the hospital. Veronica is with them. She's going to take them to my house. Curt has to stay overnight for observation. The concussive force of the blast hit him pretty hard. Curt wants me to go back to their house and see if anything is left, and if the fire department knows what happened."

Martha remembered the smell of gas floating on the air. "Could it have been a gas leak?"

"It had to be sabotage of some sort with the gas. I'd like to talk to the fire department investigator, but I don't know what they'll be willing to tell me." Daniel stood in his old jeans, smelling of smoke, with his arms crossed on his chest. Determination showed in every line from his locked jaw and tight neck muscles to his feet set squarely beneath him.

"You think if you can get close enough, you can find out what they think happened?"

"Yes. I'm sick of watching my brother's family get attacked, with nothing to do but react after the fact. I'm ready to go on the offensive, but I need information. So, I'm going to gather some intelligence first."

"Could Roberto have done this? He was at the house the day the power steering on the car was damaged. He was at the restaurant when Alegria had her allergic reaction, and he was at the house today, too." Martha brushed a strand of smoky hair out of her eyes. She was biting her lower lip, and her eyebrows were pulled together in confusion, worry, and fear.

"I don't know if Roberto did this. I want to have chat with him, though." Daniel reached out and pulled her tightly to his chest in a hug and kissed her forehead.

"We both reek of smoke." Martha laughed, almost choking on the smell from his shirt, her eyes beginning to water. "I need to take a shower."

"I have to cancel our date tonight."

Martha fought back tears that threatened to spring from her eyes. "That's understandable. Rain check?"

"Rain check." He released her from his grasp, holding onto only her hand. His amber eyes were somber as they locked onto hers.

"I know how upset you are. Try not to worry. We'll figure this out."

Before someone gets killed?

"*Yes.*"

"Can I go with you back to the house to try to get my car? Or should I leave it until later?"

Daniel put his hands on his hips and stared at the floor. "I don't know how safe it is for you to come back there. Being near my family is dangerous right now."

"The firefighters should still be there, shouldn't they? Surely with them around, we'll both be safe enough."

He conceded with a nod. "Okay."

They called a taxi and got a ride back to the smoldering remains of the Holliczek home. Barricades had been removed from the street, but yellow police tape surrounded the house. The yard was littered with charred hunks of wood and shingles. The entire front of the house was a smoldering, collapsed ruin of piles of brick and wood. Smoke still rose from somewhere in back. A firefighter retrieved an ax from the engine still in front of the house, and then sounds of chopping filled the air.

A middle-aged, paunchy, white-hatted man with a jacket labeled "Arson Inspector" stood in the yard making notes on a clipboard.

"Excuse me, sir," Daniel said. "This is my brother's house. I was here when it exploded. He's still in the hospital, but he wanted me to find out what happened."

The inspector looked up from his work and contemplated Daniel over the rim of the reading glasses he wore. "Could you answer some questions for me?" he asked in a deep, gravelly voice.

"Yes, sir," Daniel said.

"Who is this with you?" The inspector nodded his head at Martha.

"My name is Martha Rowan. That's my car by the street. I arrived here with Mrs. Holliczek right before the explosion."

"Okay," said the inspector, who then turned his attention back to Daniel, pen poised to write. "What's your full name?"

"Daniel Xavier Holliczek." He spelled out his last name.

"Your brother, Curt, and his wife, Alegria, own this property?"

"Yes."

"Had they had any work done recently on their oven, stove top, furnace, or water heater?"

"No. It definitely was a gas leak?" Daniel inched closer to the yellow tape separating him from the inspector.

"Natural gas ignited, causing the house to explode." The inspector scribbled something down and looked back up at them both.

"Is there any reason to suppose that this wasn't an accident?" Daniel lowered his voice and looked around the area, as if concerned that someone might be listening as he asked.

The inspector took a few steps closer to Daniel, moving over to the yellow tape. "Why would you ask that?"

"About three weeks ago, my brother was shot in what we think was an attempt to kidnap his one-year-old son for ransom. My sister-in-law's uncle in Peru is wealthy and has made enemies of the drug cartel down there. He received a ransom demand the day my brother was shot. The people involved in that incident were apprehended, but we still don't know who hired the kidnapper. The police think someone here gave the kidnapper information on my brother's movements. Martha witnessed the attack on Curt, and then the kidnapper tried to kill her in three separate instances. Then, last week someone punctured the power-steering reservoir in Curt and Alegria's car. Blowing up the house looks like another attack in a series of attacks."

"I see. I have a note here to call Detective Monroe. Is he in charge of the investigation?" The man's eyes were a dark smoky color and were deeply set in his head. He was still studying Martha and Curt as he asked his question.

"Yes. Detective Monroe is in charge."

"I can't give you any information. My investigation is ongoing."

"Is there anything salvageable inside the house?"

"No. The structure that remains is in danger of collapsing. I did notice some undamaged toys and tools in the back yard, but the scene is still being processed, so nothing can be removed."

Daniel's shoulders slumped. "Can I get my truck out of the driveway? It doesn't look too damaged."

Martha could see scorch marks on the front of the truck. Debris, ash, and soot coated the front hood and top. The bed of it was probably filthy, too.

The inspector glanced at the truck, still encircled by yellow tape. "Yes, you can drive it. I'll have them move the tape for you."

"Thanks." Daniel watched as the man walked approached a firefighter to ask him to move the tape.

"Did you get anything from him?" Martha asked Daniel in a whisper.

"Yes. He thinks someone tampered with the stove."

Daniel's phone rang. He looked at its screen. "It's the police," he said, and then answered. "Hello?" He paused, listening to the voice on the other end.

"Hello, Detective Monroe. No, I haven't seen Roberto since this morning. He isn't here now. No, I haven't seen Veronica yet, either. Okay, if I do, I'll let them know you'd like a word with them." Then he clicked off.

"What's up?" asked Martha.

"Roberto checked out of his hotel today. Detective Monroe couldn't get Alegria or Curt on the phone, so he called me to ask if I knew where he is."

"Roberto might have done this?" said Martha.

"I guess he could have, but why would he? I'm going to talk to him. I hope he hasn't left the country. If he checked out of his hotel, he may have had a flight out today."

"If you're going to talk to him, I'm going with you. You shouldn't go alone."

"Alegria might know Roberto's phone number. I'll call and ask her. You don't need to come with me, though. You should go home."

"You shouldn't go alone to see someone who might be a murderer."

He ran a hand through his smoky hair, dislodging some ash as he did. The ash fell in his eyes, causing him to blink rapidly to remove it. "We look like a pair of vagabonds. Go home and get cleaned up. I'll call you later."

"You are not getting rid of me that easily. If you're going to see Roberto, I'm going with you."

Daniel hung his head and stared at the debris-covered ground around them, then exhaled sharply. "Okay. I'll call Alegria for Roberto's phone number. Thanks for your help." He gave her a crooked half smile, one side of his mouth up, the other a flat line, yielding to her persistence with both exasperation and gratitude.

Chapter 17

Daniel pulled out his phone and dialed Alegria, while Martha watched the firefighters continue their work and the arson inspector continue his mapping of the ruins. The smell of smoke was heavy in the warm air, tickling Martha's nose and throat. She wanted to move away from the ruins of the Holliczek home. Visions of what the interior had looked like before the explosion floated before her eyes. The china cabinet in the dining area, the Peruvian art and decorations, and Alegria's alpaca rug flew across her mind's eye. She turned away from the wreckage of brick and wood and studied the intact homes down the street.

"Alegria isn't answering. I'll keep trying her."

Martha nodded, keeping her back to the remains of the house.

On his fourth attempt, the call went through. "Alegria?" he said. "Sorry to bother you. Are you still at the hospital? Uh-hum. Listen, do you have Roberto's number? Yes, thanks. I'll tell you why later. Veronica's there? Go to my place when they release you. I'll see you there. Yes. Okay. Bye." He ended the call, and then, already dialing, he said, "I've got Roberto's number. I'm going to try him."

Within seconds, the call was answered. "Roberto? Hi, this is Daniel Holliczek, Alegria's brother-in-law. I need to see you."

Martha waited while Daniel got directions to a hotel near DFW Airport. Finally, he ended the call and turned to her.

"Roberto switched hotels to be near the airport for his early morning flight out tomorrow. Should we take your car or my truck?"

"Both," said Martha. "We can drop my car off at my place on the way to the hotel. It's not that far out of the way. Then, on the way back, you can drop me at my apartment."

"Okay."

"Since we're going there anyway, would you mind if I run inside and change clothes? I need to wash my face and arms, too. A respectable hotel might not want me in the lobby in this condition." She held out her soot-stained arms and looked down at the stains on her once-dressy pink blouse. The blouse and the khaki capris were both smudged with soot and ash. "You could do with some washing up, too. You've got soot on your face."

"Do I?" He looked down at his clothes. "I am a mess! I don't have any spare clothes with me. You don't have anything I could borrow, do you? My place is a little out of the way."

She blushed, deep red coloring her cheeks and ears. "I might have a T-shirt you could have, one of the ones they give away free when you donate blood, or launch at you during a ball game. Those are usually too big for me."

Noting her discomposure, the twinkle returned to his eyes. "Perfect. If you don't have one, don't worry about it. I've looked and smelled worse. Soap, water, and a towel will be fine."

Forty-five minutes later, they arrived at a hotel on Highway 121 near Dallas/Fort Worth International Airport. Martha had changed at her apartment into clean jeans and green knit top and washed her face and arms, but her hair still smelled of smoke. Daniel was still wearing his old jeans and work boots, though he had brushed the ash from his hair and washed the soot from his face and arms. Martha had found a clean T-shirt big enough to fit him. She didn't tell him that she usually used it as a night shirt and made sure not to think about it when she handed it to him. The scent of soap now mingled with the smell of smoke on both of them.

They'd agreed to grab a drive-thru lunch of burgers and fries on the way to the hotel. Martha had been hungry since before leaving the mall with Alegria, hours ago. Daniel had been doing physical labor, repairing the fence all morning, and was starving as well. It was past three o'clock now and neither had eaten since breakfast. Daniel downed his burger in under a minute in the parking lot of the drive-thru before pulling his truck back onto the road. Martha ate more slowly as he drove, watching Daniel maneuver through traffic, drink his soda, and snatch fries from the bag on the console between them.

Roberto was supposed to be waiting for them in the lobby. The hotel was a simple express hotel, with a small lobby boasting a breakfast nook that served a variety of pastries and quick-cooking waffles every morning. The smell of coffee filled the air, as a full pot sat available for patrons all day long on a side counter near the heavy couch. Five stuffed chairs made up the lobby seating area. A forty-two-inch television screen tuned to a twenty-four-hour news channel dominated one wall. A talking head was presenting news and sports clips as a news scroll rolled along the bottom of the screen. The volume was low, allowing for easy conversation in the lobby and at the nearby registration desk. A subdivided rack of flyers for local attractions in Arlington, Dallas, Fort Worth, Grapevine, and a slew of other suburbs stood prominently against another wall.

Daniel spotted Roberto sitting in an overstuffed chair reading a *Dallas Morning News* and called out to him. "Roberto?"

The black-haired, mocha-skinned man looked up and smiled at them. He wore a guayabera shirt in the palest blue over white linen trousers and a pair of black, patent-leather shoes. He folded his newspaper as they approached and rose to greet them, hand outstretched to shake with Daniel.

"Hello, Daniel. It is good to see you again. And who is this?" Roberto asked with a smile at Martha, in heavily accented English. He was barely taller than Martha, maybe five feet six inches.

"This is Martha. She's a friend of mine," said Daniel. Daniel was a solid head taller, towering over the short man.

Roberto nodded and offered his hand, which Martha shook. "*Encantado*, Marta," he said, the "th" sound in her name becoming a "t" with his accent.

"What is so important that you had to see me immediately? What did you need?" Roberto asked Daniel with a puzzled look on his round, open face. The pleasant smile he had worn when he greeted them never wavered.

Daniel shifted his feet uncomfortably. "Did Veronica tell you that my brother, Curt, was shot about two weeks ago in an attempt to kidnap Felix?"

"Yes, she did. Curt told me about Alegria and Veronica's Tío Felipe dying from the shock of receiving the ransom note. He was a great old man. His loss is sadness for us all. Veronica also told me that Alegria's car was damaged. Alegria and Curt are having a run of mal de ojo."

"Well, it's more than that. Their house exploded at noon today. Someone caused a gas leak. We're all lucky we weren't killed."

"That is terrible! Someone did this on purpose? Are you sure?"

"Yes, we're sure. We're sure the shooting wasn't an accident, the car damage wasn't an accident, and the house blowing up wasn't an accident. Martha was also targeted after she saved Curt. She was shot at twice, had her apartment broken into, and was forced into a car accident."

Roberto's eyes grew two sizes in his round face as he listened to the litany of attacks. "Who can be doing this? Why?"

"We don't know. Curt was shot during an attempt to kidnap his son, Felix, but these new attacks don't have anything to do with kidnapping or ransom. They seem designed to kill. You didn't see anything when you were at the house, did you? Anyone hanging around today?"

"No, I saw nothing. I was too intent upon finishing my business with Veronica and leaving. She is very angry with me, but it is finished. We must be apart. We cannot work together anymore." He shook his head and sadness filled his eyes and face, his mouth turning down at the corners.

"Since this began with an attempt to extort money from Veronica and Alegria's Tío Felipe, we think it's about money," Daniel went on. "Do you know of anyone in Peru who might need money badly enough to try to kidnap my nephew?"

"Veronica and I are both short of cash right now, with the business closed down, but we both have properties to fall back on if we need money in the future." A startled look followed by anger flashed across his round face. "Did you come here to ask me if I did this?" He looked at Daniel with disbelief, his mouth wrinkling up with distaste, as if he'd smelled or tasted something unsavory.

"I'm sorry, but you were at the house the day the car was sabotaged and today, right before the house blew up. You arrived in the country not long after Curt was attacked. I had to see you, even if only to rule you out as a suspect." Daniel held his hand out to shake in an offering of peace and apology.

Roberto hesitated, but took it. "I understand. I would do the same in your position. You said no one was killed today. Was anyone injured? Why is Curt not here questioning me?"

"He got a concussion and is at the hospital for observation. Alegria is there, too. She got knocked pretty hard by the explosion. Felix is okay, maybe a little bruised."

"I see. I am sorry. In your shoes, I would be questioning everyone, too. I have no answers for you, other than I did not do any of this. I hope you discover the guilty party soon."

The conversation drew to an uncomfortable close. Martha and Daniel said their goodbyes and left.

"Did you read his thoughts?" asked Martha, as they got in the car for the drive back to Carrollton.

"Yes. Either he's really good at masking his thoughts, or he doesn't know a thing about it. His main concern right now is his break-up with Veronica. He's worried about her and upset by how angry she is with him. The thought crossed his mind that she might be behind this, but he dismissed it pretty quickly."

"What now?"

"First, we'll get you home. Then, I'm going to call Detective Monroe and tell him where to find Roberto. I'm going back to my house to get Alegria and Felix settled. We probably need to go buy a bunch of new stuff, like a crib for Felix."

Silence fell between them.

Martha forced herself to think about the problems of rebuilding and restocking an entire house so that she wouldn't think about how attracted she was to Daniel or dwell on their canceled date. The unknown identity of the person behind all the attacks began to trouble her again.

What if we never find out who did all this?

"*We will. The police will solve it, or we will figure it out.*"

"Daniel, don't do that!"

"Sorry." He looked over at her and grinned, amber eyes twinkling. "I keep forgetting you can hear me answer."

Martha knew he hadn't forgotten at all. He was teasing her. She smiled back at him, wanting to reach out and touch him, but not brave enough to do it.

"If Roberto is innocent, could one of Alegria's cousins, a secondary heir, be after her uncle's trust fund money? These things usually go back to money, don't they?" asked Martha.

"If it's a vendetta of some sort, no, but if we exclude vendettas, then I'd agree. Money is a motivating factor in most crime. A cousin in Peru could have hired someone to keep attacking Curt and Alegria."

"Could Alegria call her family in Peru and ask a few questions? Surely someone there must have some idea. If someone is deeply in debt and needs money, wouldn't debt collectors be calling like they do here? Someone would have noticed if a relative had financial problems, wouldn't they?"

"I would hope so. I'll ask her to call her mother and her aunts. Making calls will give her some distraction while we wait to hear from the insurance adjuster," said Daniel.

They arrived at Martha's Carrollton apartment complex ten minutes later. Daniel walked Martha down the sidewalk past the prickly holly bushes to her door, gave her a quick kiss on the cheek, and stood back as she went inside. She watched him vanish down the sidewalk back to the parking area before closing her door.

Chapter 18

Showered, changed into fresh walking shorts and a sleeve-less T-shirt with sandals, and smelling of lavender instead of soot, Martha took her car to a car wash. She sat inside the air-conditioned building and watched through an enormous window as employees wiped down the interior and exterior by hand. Luckily, the wax job on the new car made the cleaning easier.

Her phone began to ring in her pocket.

"Hello?"

"Hi, Martha. It's Bill. I saw a news report on a house blow-ing up. The owners were reported injured in the blast, and the name I heard was Holliczek. Do you know if that's the same Holliczek family?"

"It is. I was there."

"You were there! Are you okay?"

"Yes. I'm getting the soot and ash washed off my car. The house is a total loss. The family will be staying with Daniel now. He's gone to get supplies and things for them."

"The news reported a gas explosion. It wasn't an accident, was it?"

"We don't think so."

"Someone wants to hurt this family. Heidi's with me. Hold on. She has a question."

Heidi came on the line. "Hi, Martha, is there anything I can do to help? They probably need to buy all new things."

"I know they'll need new stuff. If you wanted to get stuff for the baby, I'm sure they'd appreciate it. Do you want me to ask them, or do you want to surprise them?" asked Martha.

"I'll put together a basket for them. How old is the baby?"

"He turned one a couple weeks ago. Thanks, Heidi, that's sweet of you."

"Martha, Bill here again. Are they doing anything about protection?"

"If they knew who was behind this, they could protect themselves. As it is, I don't know what they can do."

"I suppose it doesn't help to arm yourself against someone exploding your house. Well, Heidi will give you a call when she gets her basket of goodies in order. Take care."

Martha ended the call and put her phone away. She wished she were out on a date with Daniel. However, given the circumstances, she felt guilty that she was sad to be missing a date. Heidi had the right idea. Don't sit. Do something to help. Alegria would need all sorts of things. Martha couldn't replace Alegria's Peruvian art or alpaca rug, but she could get kitchen supplies, towels, and clothes for Felix. Tonight she would shop. Tomorrow, after church, she could deliver the items she would buy.

As MARTHA ARRIVED home that evening, lugging bags of children's toys, bath towels, and kitchen items from her shopping spree, her phone rang.

"Hi, Martha, it's Daniel."

Her heart beat faster as she dropped the bags she was carrying on the living room floor.

"Hi," she said breathlessly.

"You okay?" he asked.

"Yes, I was carrying some stuff. I decided since Curt and Alegria need all new stuff, I'd help them get started on the shopping."

"Did you? You didn't have to do that! Alegria will be thrilled, though. She's been fretting all afternoon over what to do. She's called the insurance company already, and they'll be coming to check the scene. The place is a total loss, so she and Curt will have to knock it down and rebuild. I've been attempting to convince her that they can stay here until the new house is rebuilt."

"Not that I'd want to do it on these terms, but designing a new house might be fun."

"That's what I told her. She's always wanted more kitchen cabinets and a bigger pantry. Veronica's infuriated with Roberto. She's mad enough about the way the business has been split up that she wants to tear him limb from limb. She blamed him for the house, the car damage, Curt's attack, and every other thing that has gone wrong in the history of civilization."

"Did you tell Detective Monroe where to find Roberto?"

"Yes. He'll definitely see Roberto before he leaves the country. He's already interviewed Veronica."

"Great. Can I bring Alegria the things I bought tomorrow?"

"Absolutely. I'll give you a tour of my house."

"What time do you want me to come?"

"Will three o'clock work? The hospital is keeping Curt overnight for observation because of his head injury, but we expect he'll be released before noon. If they're late releasing him, I want to leave some margin for error."

"Three o'clock is great."

"Martha, I'm sorry about not being able to take you to the play tonight."

"Daniel, I'm disappointed we didn't get to go, but I know you have a lot to do for Curt and Alegria. I'd feel guilty if I pulled you away from that. Besides, we can try again. Remember, you said I could have a rain check."

"You are wonderful. Listen, Felix started crying. He must be getting hungry, and Alegria's at the hospital checking on Curt. I have to go. I'll see you tomorrow. Bye."

"Bye."

Martha sat down to a snack at her kitchen table and contemplated the unknown cousins who might want to harm Curt and Alegria. Could they hire people to come here and do all these things? Damage a car's power steering? Blow up a house? If they needed money, how would they pay someone for all of that? Surely hiring a hit man cost a lot.

The phone rang again, interrupting her pondering of the situation.

"Hi, Martha, it's Heidi. I have a package of things to deliver to the Holliczek family. I was wondering if you could tell me where to deliver it?"

"Yes, I can, but I liked your idea so much that I went and bought some things, too. How would you like to come with me to deliver all the things at once?"

"Perfect. Where should we meet?" Heidi asked.

"You can come to my apartment. It would be on the way south for you."

"What time?"

"Two-thirty?"

"Okay. See you then."

Martha watched television, put the gifts she'd purchased into gift bags, and did a load of smoke-scented laundry.

She went to bed certain that she would never get to sleep, got up and took a dose of the medicine the doctor had prescribed, and crawled back into bed with a book. Martha slept soundly in spite of her brain.

Sunday dawned bright. Dressing early in white capri pants and a sleeveless, lavender-colored blouse with a matching short-sleeved sweater and white, low-heeled sandals, Martha attended church and then treated herself to a grilled cheese sandwich lunch. The hours before two-thirty flew by with reading and whiling away time on the computer.

Martha heard a knock on her door and looked through the peephole to see Heidi and Bill standing on her doorstep.

"Hi," she said as she opened the door. "Let me grab my things, and you can follow me there." She handed Bill a slip of paper with a map on it. "Here's a map and Daniel's address. He lives in Plano."

"We'll follow you." Bill was in his weekend casual clothes, dressed in jeans, this time with a red-checkered, short-sleeved, button-down shirt with his Rangers ball cap over his head.

"Can we help carry anything?" Heidi asked as Martha picked up three large gift bags of items. Heidi wore a skirt in an orange-and-yellow floral print with a matching orange pullover top. She had yellow, ballerina-style shoes on her feet.

"No, thanks, I've got it," said Martha.

They arrived outside a square brick house with pale-yellow trim on a large lot in a quiet neighborhood that dated back to the 1980s. The neighboring houses were mostly square, exhibiting three or four different floor plans at the most, but differentiated by their owners with paint, landscaping, and window boxes. In most of the houses, the garages had been converted into extra rooms. Some conversions were more professional than others, with French doors or bay windows where the garage doors had been. A few do-it-yourselfers had simply walled over the area. A variety of decorative mailboxes stood by the road in front of each house. Daniel's now-clean truck was parked in the narrow driveway that led to his unconverted single-car garage.

Martha, Heidi, and Bill carried their gifts to the doorway and knocked. No one answered. Martha rang the bell. They waited, arms growing tired under the burden of gifts. Still, no one answered.

"Did they know we were coming?" Bill asked as he stepped back off the porch and surveyed the front of the house.

"Yes. I spoke to Daniel. He said they'd be here," Martha said. She hesitated to follow Bill back off the porch. Warning bells began to chime in her head and the hair on her neck prickled. Something was wrong.

"I hope nothing more has happened," said Heidi. She turned around and looked at the neighboring houses. No one was out in the afternoon heat. No cars approached. Sunday afternoon silence reined.

"Let me try his cell phone," Martha said. She set her bags at her feet.

Martha dialed, but the call went to voice mail. She left a short message.

A moment later she heard Daniel's voice as clearly as if he were standing next to her.

"Call the police. Get help!"

"Bill, something is terribly wrong." Martha looked in the window by the door, but could see no one.

"Be careful. Gun."

"Let's put this stuff in the car." She trotted back to the cars, Bill and Heidi following more slowly in her wake.

Martha flung the gifts into the trunk of her car and studied the front of the house. No movement was visible. "I can't explain it, but I think we need to call the police. Heidi, can you call that Detective Monroe, while Bill and I check around back? Here's his number." Martha pulled the detective's card from her wallet and handed it to Heidi. "Stay down and out of sight. I don't want anyone shot today."

"Shot?" Bill asked, alarmed. The questions in his eyes were deepening into concern. He looked her up and down, trying to decide whether she was overreacting.

"Call it sixth sense, but something is wrong. Do you think we could peek in the back or side windows?" She knew he wasn't convinced of the need. "Please."

"If you want, I'll go with you." He still wasn't convinced, Martha knew, but at least he was willing to investigate.

"Try and stay low, so we won't be seen by anyone inside."

"Okay." Bill gave her a puzzled look, but cooperated.

Martha ducked behind the cars and then behind Daniel's truck, and made her way to the side of the house next to the driveway. Bill stooped down and followed behind her. They passed a running air-conditioning condensing unit and arrived at a six-foot-tall wooden fence with a gate that looked newly replaced. Martha eased the gate open as quietly as she could. It swung easily on new hinges. That side of the house was solid brick and had no windows.

Staying low, Martha peeked around the brick corner of the house into the large back yard. Shaded by the rough-barked, black-brown branches of an ancient mesquite tree draped heavily with immature green mesquite beans, the St. Augustine grass in the yard grew thick. No signs of any occupants appeared. A two-foot-wide window allowed light into the back corner of the house. The bottom of the window would have been at Martha's waist if she had been standing. She crawled under the brick ledge at the bottom of the window, staying as close to the wall as possible, followed closely by Bill. As Martha reached the corner of the window, she heard muffled words coming from inside. A baby's wailing cry ended any chance of understanding the words.

Martha peeked her head up enough to see into one corner of the window before snatching her head back and plastering herself to the wall under the window. Daniel, Curt, Alegria, Veronica and Felix were all in the dining area at the back of the house. Alegria cradled the fussy baby in her arms, bouncing him lightly. Daniel stood facing the window, his hands raised before him. Curt stood by the dining table, placing items into a pillow case. Veronica stood directly in front of the window with her back to it.

Martha tried to stop the shaking that had begun in her hands and knees. She took a deep breath before leaning over and whispering in Bill's ear. "Bill, she's got a gun."

"Mrs. Holliczek?" he whispered back.

"No, it's her sister."

"Are they facing this window? Can we signal them without being seen?" he whispered in her ear as the sounds of arguing voices rose from inside the house. Someone silenced the baby mid-cry, maybe with a sippy cup or pacifier.

"Yes, they're right inside the window. If she turns around and sees us, I don't know what she'll do." They stopped talking and pressed closer to the wall as the voices grew louder.

Veronica's heavily accented voice floated through the glass, only slightly muffled. She sound like a queen, imperious and demanding that her orders be followed. "Do as I said! Put the jewelry and the electronics, phones, tablets, and laptop in the pillow case. This is going to look like you were killed in a robbery."

"Veronica, if you needed money, you could have asked me. We would have helped!" said Alegria. She was hurt and confused and sounded as if she was ready to argue with her sister, regardless of the gun in Veronica's hand. Her accent was getting heavier with each word. Martha hoped they didn't switch to Spanish.

"Alegria, you can't even afford a maid or a nanny. You could not possibly have the amount of money I need to clear up my financial problems. If I miss another payment, I will lose two properties. I will lose my position on the bank board. I will lose my place in the community. I need Tío Felipe's money, and I need it now." Veronica's voice was calm and steady, and seemed absent of any distress over what she was doing.

"Then why not get a loan from Tío Felipe? He would have lent you whatever you needed. You could have repaid him once you sold some property. Instead, you scared him to death and gave him a heart attack. Why?" Alegria's voice was loud, clear, and angry. Felix whimpered in her arms.

"Do you think I want everyone to know about my problems? To think I was a poor business woman, incapable of taking care of my own accounts? My colleagues would lose respect for me. My position in the community would be weakened. People on the board at the bank might have started voting against my plans. No one can know. No one will know."

"You would have kidnapped my baby and killed my husband, all so you wouldn't lose face with your friends! Are you crazy?! Felix and Curt could have died!" Alegria was yelling now.

"No one was supposed to get hurt. If that stupid woman hadn't interfered, it would all have gone smoothly," said Veronica.

"No one was supposed to get hurt? What about Tío Felipe? You should have known the shock could give him a heart attack! He'd already had two previous attacks."

"I had to take that chance." Veronica sounded bored. "Hurry up with those things! I have a plane to catch tonight, and I still have to pack."

Alegria wasn't done. "You volunteered to watch Felix instead of letting Curt taking him to work that morning. Did you change your mind at the last minute?"

"No! I would not be so weak. Curt was so excited about showing Felix off to his coworkers, I knew he would never agree to let me babysit. I realized I would look innocent in the aftermath if my actions almost prevented the whole incident. Even the detective didn't see that possibility. I never wanted Felix hurt, if I could avoid it. I made sure to keep him home with me when I damaged the car steering. Only when more subtle methods failed did I resort to things that would endanger him as well. I would be an excellent mother to him in Peru. He will have everything he needs."

"What do you mean?" asked Curt.

"Shut up and put the whole jewelry box inside," said Veronica.

"You would kill us and take Felix?" Alegria asked.

"He is too young to remember anything or be a witness against me. I have no reason to kill him. People would admire me for taking in my poor orphaned nephew. Perhaps, then, Roberto would be satisfied with raising him, and not insist that I have children. I do not have time for pregnancy. Roberto might come back to me. My refusal to have children was always a bigger matter to him than our business problems."

"You are crazy!" Alegria screamed.

Bill and Martha crouched against the cool brick wall under the window and listened. Martha was aghast at what she heard. Her heart beat quick and heavy in her throat, and her breathing was shallow. Bill put his hand on her shoulder and nodded his head toward the corner of the house to say, "Come with me back around the house."

Martha shook her head no. She whispered, "Go tell Heidi to tell the police that they're being held at gunpoint. I'll try and get a signal to the others that we're here."

He nodded and crawled back around the corner of the house, knees getting stained green by the St. Augustine grass.

Martha listened to a blue jay calling from the tree and the wind blowing in her ears. She closed her eyes to block out the noises of the yard and distant traffic. Praying silently that Daniel was close enough to hear her, she focused on him, willing her thoughts to go out.

Daniel, I'm here. Can you hear me?

"Yes. Where are you?"

Back of the house, under the window. Bill and Heidi are calling the police. What can I do?

"Cause a distraction."

No! Last time I did that Curt got shot! Can't we wait for the police?

"I don't know how long we've got until she gets tired of arguing with Alegria. Cause a distraction, and we can take her down."

You'll get shot! No!

"Two against one this time. I'm going to tackle her, and Curt's going to get the gun. We won't get shot. Promise. Cause a distraction! Please!"

Okay! I'm looking.

Martha looked around, frantically searching for anything to use to cause a distraction. Round concrete stepping stones in the process of being swallowed by grass formed a path from the back porch to the side of the house, leading to the outdoor water spigot. One stone was broken into three large segments.

Hang on. I see a way, but I need a minute.

"Hurry."

Alegria's angry voice floated through the window glass in rapid-fire Spanish. Martha couldn't understand a word of what she was saying. Veronica yelled something back equally rapidly in Spanish. Hopefully, Veronica would be inclined to argue a little longer.

Staying low, Martha crawled over to the stepping stones. She ripped off the vining runners of St. Augustine that were engulfing the stone, and dug her fingers into the surrounding dark soil. She yanked and wiggled, praying under her breath that she would be fast enough. At last, she pried a chunk of the broken concrete out of the ground, exposing slimy, brown earthworms and ants to the air. Thanking God that they weren't fire ants, Martha brushed the ants from the stone and off of her fingers. With dirt under her nails and the rock in hand, she skittered back under the window.

Daniel, I'm going to break the window with a chunk of concrete.

"Okay. We're ready."

1, 2, 3, now!

Aiming for the unscreened, upper half of the window, Martha launched the concrete wedge toward the back of Veronica's head. The concrete demolished the window, shattering the glass inward. Martha ducked back down, her knees shaking, and didn't see whether the rock had struck Veronica or not. A scream erupted from inside the house. Multiple car doors slammed somewhere in front of the house as a gun fired inside. Felix started wailing, a loud, scared cry that echoed through the room and out the broken window.

A huge bang combined with the splintering of wood at the front of the house was followed by shouts of "Police! Put your hands up!"

Chapter 19

Martha told the police a version of truth that had nothing to do with direct mental communication between her, Daniel, and Curt. Instead, she said she'd felt uneasy given all that had already happened when no one answered the door. She explained that the lack of response had prompted her to go around back and peek in the window. She'd seen Veronica holding the gun and signaled Daniel and Curt to tell them she would break the window. They had used the distraction to wrestle the gun out of Veronica's hands. The gun had fired as Veronica hit the ground, having been tackled by Daniel, sending a bullet into the floorboard on the bottom of the wall.

Veronica was taken into custody. Martha's last view of her came as Veronica sat rigidly in the back of a police car, staring straight ahead, refusing to make eye contact with her sister Alegria. Curt had to gently pull the crying Alegria away from the police car as it rolled away.

Three days later, Alegria, Curt, and Daniel gave Bill, Heidi, and Martha the rest of the details over a feast of fajitas, grilled vegetables, and flour tortillas at one of the ubiquitous Tex-Mex restaurants in Dallas.

"After the house exploded, Alegria called her family in Peru and asked questions about who might be in financial trouble. A little digging turned up that Veronica was deeply in debt, having purchased property that she couldn't sell quickly enough to meet her cash flow demands," Daniel explained.

"Since her business has been virtually closed down by the divorce proceedings, she had no cash coming in."

"When I approached her about whether she needed money, Veronica denied everything at first," Alegria said, slowly and soberly. "But I kept asking her questions, and she stormed out of the house. A few minutes later, she came back with a gun. She must have had it hidden in the car. Veronica told us she needed the money, and if we had to die for her to get it, so be it. She decided to shoot us and make it look like a robbery. She'd already planned to fly back to Peru tonight." Alegria stopped talking as her voice cracked. Tears formed at the corners of her eyes, and she dabbed them away carefully with a delicate handkerchief that she seemed to be clutching for emotional support.

Curt took up the story for his choked-up wife. "Her original plan was to extort what she needed from her uncle. She hired Rios, who, in turn, hired thugs to eliminate Martha. Veronica didn't plan on her uncle's death. Then, she had to improvise a new plan to get cash to pay her debts. She'd inherited land from him, which she couldn't sell fast enough to meet her needs. She wanted the cash from the trust fund."

"I can't believe she would hurt you all. She appeared to care for Felix so much," Martha said. The sleeping child snuggled against his mother, his head of tangled, light brown hair lolling sideways on her shoulder, one tiny hand grasping a handful of her shiny black hair.

Alegria nodded in agreement. "If she could have arranged to kill only me and Curt, she wanted to be the one to raise Felix, and get control of the funds being left to him. Even today, she said she wouldn't shoot him, since he is too young to remember anything. She doesn't know the meaning of love. She saw Felix as a useful accessory, something to reflect well on her and bring her money. When the ransom scheme failed and my uncle died a few days later, she knew she needed a new plan. She waited until Curt came home from the hospital. Then she damaged the steering on my car to try to kill us. She thought she would control the trust fund and get to take care of Felix if we died, so she volunteered to babysit that night. I never told her that if something happens to us, according to the wills we made right after Felix was born, we've left care of the baby and his finances to Daniel." Alegria laughed out loud, tears still in her eyes, as her somber mood was lightened by the look of shock on Daniel's face. "See, you don't know everything!"

"I had no idea you were considering me for raising Felix!" Daniel said.

"Well, relax! We don't intend for you to ever have to fulfill that need," said Curt. "We hope to be here to raise him ourselves."

"I'm going to have to take better care of you two," Daniel said. "That kid is a handful."

"Do you think she planned all along to take Felix in hopes of satisfying Roberto's desire for children? Or did she think of that later?" asked Martha.

"I'm not sure when that occurred to her. She wasn't thinking about that when the house blew up. Felix could have been killed along with the rest of us. Her main goal was the cash in the trust fund," said Curt.

"What about the incident in the other restaurant? Your allergic reaction?" asked Martha. "Did she cause that, too?"

"It's possible. She did leave the table right before the food was delivered. I don't think we will ever be able to prove that," Alegria said. "It's strange to think that she would do this. As a child, she was difficult. The nanny used to give up and let her have her way rather than argue with her. She had such a stubborn streak and a driving desire to get her own way. I knew she thought her ways were better than everyone else's, but I didn't realize she completely disregarded the value of other people and their opinions. She would rearrange things to suit herself without regard to how it affected anyone else, like the cabinets and drawers in my house. I knew she could be terribly self-centered, but I didn't realize she was so ... What was the word in English, Curt?"

"Narcissistic." Curt put his arm around his wife's shoulders and pulled her and his son to him. He kissed them both lightly, Alegria on the cheek and the baby on the top of his tangled hair. He picked up where Alegria left off. "When all of that failed, Veronica turned on all the burners on the stove without lighting the gas, so the gas leaked into the house. When I opened the door, I smelled it. I'm not sure what sparked it off. She must have rigged something to spark. Maybe the arson inspector will figure it out. After that, she was running out of time, so she pulled the gun on us."

"And Roberto? Did he know anything about this?" asked Martha.

"No, I called him on the phone and caught him right after his flight landed in Peru. When I told him what Veronica had done, he was speechless," Curt said. "He said she was horribly self-centered, but he didn't think she was this crazy. He's lucky she didn't decide to kill him to solve her problems."

"Maybe she thought she could win him back. Maybe she really loved him," said Heidi.

"She may have wanted to win him back, but I doubt she knows how to love anyone. He had the assets to their business, which she wanted. He also met her need to look like the perfect couple. Appearances were important to her," said Alegria. "She hoped to get her hands on Felix and reunite with Roberto, and complete her picture of a perfect family to present to her friends and neighbors."

The meal ended peacefully, and they all walked outside the restaurant together.

"Well, I would say it's been nice meeting you," said Bill, as he and Heidi prepared to leave after dinner, "but, I hope I never have to see a situation like that again."

"Believe me, Sir, so do we," said Curt as he shook Bill's outstretched hand.

"Thank you so much for the things you bought for us. You are so generous and sweet," said Alegria, as she hugged and air kissed both Heidi and Bill.

Bill turned to Daniel and shook his hand, saying, "Call me if you want help replacing that front door. The police did a pretty thorough job knocking it down."

"I think I can handle it, but thanks for the offer," said Daniel.

"See you tomorrow, Martha," said Bill, as Heidi gave Martha a hug goodbye.

Bill and Heidi waved goodbye and vanished around the corner of the restaurant to where they had parked their car.

"I've been waiting all evening for Bill and Heidi to leave so that I could ask you a question," Martha said to Daniel. "You can hear people's thoughts. How come you didn't know Veronica was behind all the attacks?"

"I wasn't living in the same house with her. When I did go to Curt and Alegria's house, she would be in the guest room or helping with Felix. I overheard her thinking about her divorce and how she thought Alegria needed a maid. Honestly, we avoided each other for the most part. I didn't like her very much, and I got the impression that she didn't care for me. She may even have avoided me on purpose." He turned to Alegria. "She knew I could hear people thinking, didn't she?"

"Yes. However, she didn't like you very much when she met you last year, so she avoided you," Alegria said with a laugh and a twinkle in her eye. "She told me that she didn't like the idea of anyone hearing her thinking. That handsome face of yours can't charm everyone."

"Her avoidance would have made me suspect her, except she always avoided me whenever we met. Last time she visited, I don't think I spoke ten words to her. This time was no different. We didn't suspect her until Alegria called Peru and learned about her financial problems," said Daniel. "Though, since she was planning on flying out tonight, she must have known she couldn't stay in the same house with me for very long before I heard her think something about her plans. That's probably what precipitated today's madness, more than Alegria questioning her. She knew she was out of time."

"I don't know how I am going to tell my mother about all this. She will be devastated. We will have to get Veronica a lawyer," said Alegria sadly.

"She did try to kill us all several times, you know," Curt said.

"I know, but she is my sister. We should see if she needs anything while she is in jail. I will go see her tomorrow," Alegria said.

"You have a good heart," said Curt, squeezing her to him, his arm around her shoulder.

A half-moon glowed in the night sky, which was devoid of any visible stars, obscured by ambient light from the city. A fluffy white cloud or two drifted across the dark canopy. The warm air was still, but not stifling since the sun had gone down. The parking lot and cars still radiated heat absorbed by the metal and concrete during the daylight hours.

Daniel walked Martha to her car, and looked over his shoulder at Curt and Alegria waiting for him under the lights of the restaurant. He grimaced at them and turned his attention to Martha. "Thanks for coming. You saved us all again," he said.

"All I did was cause a distraction, which you told me to do. You saved yourselves. By the way, I heard you from the front of the house today. We should test how far you can project yourself mentally sometime. I'd also like to know exactly how far away you have to be to not hear me thinking."

"I can yell mentally farther than I can hear, remember?" he said, eyes aglow with mischief.

"Yes." Martha's eyes locked again on those beautiful, twinkling amber eyes. She didn't know if she'd ever get used to that charming smile and those gorgeous eyes.

"I hope you will."

Daniel stepped closer and kissed Martha on the lips, gently at first and then harder, before hugging her close to him.

Applause and a loud whistle from Curt rang across the parking lot outside the restaurant.

Daniel rolled his eyes. "I'll call you tomorrow. We *will* get to go out on a normal date, where no one gets shot at or blown up. I promise." He smiled at her, then turned and trotted back across the parking lot to where Alegria and Curt were waiting for him.

Epilogue

Three days later, Martha sat in the psychiatrist's office for her appointment. The office was comfortable and private, a one-person operation without even a receptionist. A doorbell rang when the outer door that led to a tiny waiting area was opened. The doctor himself came out of his interior office to greet her. Soft classical music played in the waiting area to cover any voices from the interior office, should patients arrive early for an appointment while the doctor was still with someone. The chair Martha sat on was comfortable, but plain. One wall of the office was covered with bookshelves full of reference materials and books on health and the mind. An ornate antique wall clock was centered on the back wall over a printer sitting on a small cabinet.

The conversation was going well. The doctor was congenial and well spoken. He'd given her suggestions of articles to read about post-traumatic stress and the recovery process for it. His suggestions showed he recognized and respected her intelligence and gave her credit for being ready and willing to do the work that needed to be done to improve her condition.

"Well, Miss Rowan. We have a bit of work ahead of us, but you can get through this. I understand your concerns with the medication. You can taper off using it as we progress with your other therapies. I'll give you a schedule of how to stop taking the medicine when it's time. First, we'll work on some strategies to change your thinking patterns with what's called cognitive behavior therapy. We can integrate a few other techniques if you aren't making progress, but the cognitive therapy will help a great deal."

"That sounds good to me."

"I'm going to teach you a couple techniques to practice today. Before we start, I want to give you some paperwork to fill out. These are questionnaires that will give me a better understanding of your mental state. I have to say, based on our conversation, that PTSD might not be the only issue here. Anxiety has been an issue for you for a long time, hasn't it?"

"Yes," she admitted.

"Fill these out and return them to me before your next appointment. I'll review your answers, and we can discuss the results at your next appointment," said the doctor.

Martha nodded and accepted the thick manila packet of papers. "I'll get these back to you as soon as possible."

"Wonderful. Now, are you ready to answer some questions?"

"Okay, Doctor. Let's get started."

About the Author

N. M. CEDEÑO lives and writes near Austin, Texas. A native Texan, she has also lived in Houston, Dallas, and Amarillo. N. M. Cedeño writes both short stories and novels. Her work falls mainly in the mystery genre and includes traditional mysteries, suspense, and science fiction mysteries set in the near future.

TO CONNECT WITH N. M. CEDEÑO

For additional information about upcoming stories and novels or to connect with the author, please visit nmcedeno.com.